AFTERWARDS

David Kennedy

Raider Publishing International

New York   London   Cape Town

© 2010 David Kennedy

All rights reserved. No part of this book may be reproduced stored in a retrieval system or transmitted in any form by any means with out the prior written permission of the publisher, except by a reviewer who may quote brief passages in a review to be printed in a newspaper, magazine or journal.

First Printing

The views, content and descriptions in this book do not represent the views of Raider Publishing International. Some of the content may be offensive to some readers and they are to be advised. Objections to the content in this book should be directed towards the author and owner of the intellectual property rights as registered with their local government.

All characters portrayed in this book are fictitious and any resemblance to persons living or dead is purely coincidental.

Cover images courtesy of istockphoto.com

ISBN: 978-1-61667-118-1

Published By Raider Publishing International
www.RaiderPublishing.com
New York London Cape Town
Printed in the United States of America and the United Kingdom

In memory of David Kennedy, my father, and Liz Kennedy, my sister.

This book was inspired by the paintings of William Blake, the music of Krzystof Penderecki, and some blank pages of infinity.

AFTERWARDS

David Kennedy

Contents

CHAPTER   PAGE

5. *My Decision*..1
4. *The State* 15
3. *My Family*..29
2. *Freedom Day*..43
1. *My Final Day*..57
0. *Afterwards* 71

If you don't like it here, go back to where you came from.

KILGORE TROUT, *TIMEQUAKE*

5
My Decision

I CAN REMEMBER WHEN I MADE THE DECISION TO END IT ALL. It was a special day for me, but, as I awoke, I could not remember what that special day was. There was definitely something in the air, that once in a lifetime kind of thing that you are meant to remember for the rest of your life. I couldn't quite think straight about what that thing was, so I lay in bed silently looking up at the ceiling. I followed the cracks, which silently evolved above my head, moving as I slept. I had been doing this for quite a while up until today, though I couldn't remember if it was seconds, minutes, days, hours, months or years that I'd been looking above me every morning, following the cracks along their way. That's the way my life went, up until that fateful day.

I also enjoyed looking around the edges of the walls where they met the ceiling. I liked the straight lines, and I loved to watch the little black squiggles in front of my eyes darting along in straight lines like waves. As I moved my eyes faster and faster along the edges of the walls, the little black squiggles shot farther out of my line of vision, then sank down as I rested my gaze at a point above me. This was a great way to start the day.

So I was lying there looking up above me, and then I realised it was my birthday. I don't know how I remembered it was my birthday; it was just one of those things that came around in my head as I was moving my eyes frantically. I think I was thinking along the lines of what I had to eat in the fridge, then, eureka, I remembered it was my birthday, and then it got me thinking about how old I was. Now I was never going to forget how old I was; it was a once in a lifetime age. So I thought about that for another few seconds, and realised I was fifty years old; half a century had passed by me. *Wow*!

I found I was finding it hard to remember all those years that had passed. To be honest, I couldn't remember anything much after the last ten years; nothing much had changed, and nothing much had happened to me. I can remember spending a lot of time sleeping, though I think a lot of people also do this. I can remember eating a lot— well, we all have to do that— and thinking about everything. In fact, I can remember thinking so much about everything that I didn't want to think any longer about the way things had panned out for me, so I can distinctly remember one day, must have been ten years before this day, my fiftieth birthday, that I would try to not think about how things had gone for me and why I spent my time waking up looking at ceilings and not wanting to think about things.

So, I must have been forty when I decided to stop thinking about things. Forty! That was ten years ago. I can remember looking up at the ceiling on my fiftieth birthday, thinking about my fortieth birthday, and thinking that was ten years ago; it couldn't have been ten years ago, could it? I tried hard to picture ten years in my head as a kind of space in my life. Well, ten years was a fifth of my life, and I visualised a kind of pie chart where one fifth of the pie chart was filled with a pink colour and the other four fifths were filled a blue colour. This pie chart made bad reading for me, and I can remember lying there with my eyes closed looking at the pie chart, and thinking, *where the hell did the ten years of pink go to?*

I opened my eyes and threw back the covers on my bed. My thin body sat scrawny on the mattress; the same mattress I'd had for quite a while now. Well, if I can remember correctly, I bought this mattress when I was moved into this house, so, to my surprise, I must have had this mattress over thirteen years. It surprised me greatly that I could be sleeping on the same bed for thirteen years, and that I could be resting my bones on the same mattress for thirteen years, so that means I must have been waking up looking at the cracks in the ceiling for thirteen years. I was very surprised at this amount of time passing me by. I tried to make a pie chart of thirteen years from fifty; I could do the colouring; this time, the small pie would be coloured red, and the large portion of the pie, green. I couldn't actually work out the exact proportions of the pie, but I knew the small portion would be slightly larger in this pie chart than the last one I had just imagined regarding my fifty years of being alive, so I guessed it. It worked fine for me, lying in bed with no one else around to correct me if I was wrong.

So, then, I thought, *if I'm fifty, it means I was born in...* I thought about it for a second. *2049, which means it is 2099, which means it is only six days until the start of a new century.* I can remember feeling excited about this, as I always did on my birthday. I was always more excited about Christmas and the New Year, rather than my birthday; I don't remember why, so I can only think that birthdays aged you more. I mean, you never ask people 'how many Christmases have you had', or 'how many New Years' days have you seen come and go'. Birthdays had a definite age to them and, for some reason or other, you very rarely forgot that age; it was always with you, stuck in the back of your mind somewhere, so, even if you didn't remember as soon as you woke up, you would remember pretty quickly just afterward. So I worked it out that I was born on the twenty-sixth of December 2049. My mother used to say I was born at nearly ten to nine. I never laughed at that joke, and never would. I remember thinking about my mother lying there thinking about the ceiling. It meant that I hadn't seen my mother for thirteen years; this number, thirteen, was beginning to creep up a lot on me. So I began thinking about the number thirteen and about how it had been an unlucky number in certain parts of the world. The world was strange, because certain things in some parts of the world didn't mean the same in other parts of the world, like the number thirteen and, even though the world relied on the people of the world getting along and living in peace and harmony, these different things did not mean the same thing around the globe. This confused me greatly, and I made the decision to get out of bed.

I sat up in bed to the four bare walls of the bedroom. It was a small square room with a one-pane window at the side of my bed. My legs felt weak when I placed my weight on them, and I can remember thinking, *When was the last time I had actually used my legs to walk anywhere?* It could have been anywhere from two days to two hours; I just couldn't remember, at the time, when I felt the carpet fibres pressing against the soles of my feet. I instantly felt dizzy, so I rested a little and sat on the side of the bed, my feet looking like a couple of tents and the green carpet in the bedroom a field in the summer sunshine. I felt instantly better at this thought and stood; this time, I bore the weight well and went over to the window; this was the first thing I did every morning, afternoon or evening when I woke up— go over to the window and open the vertical blinds to see what kind of a morning, afternoon or evening it was. It was dark outside, so that instantly made me realise that this was either the evening or the morning; it being the winter, it was always dark in the morning and evenings.

The cars all hovered by in straight lines by my window thirty floors below. They all disappeared into the distance, all of them travelling at the regulatory twenty-five miles per hour. In my house, by the way, it was built so that I could only see the traffic going away from the building, and I couldn't honestly remember the last time I had ever seen the traffic coming towards my window. Thinking about how long it had been since I had seen the traffic coming toward me, I ventured to find out what time it was; well, rather, what time of day it was, morning or evening.

I walked out the small bedroom with the green carpet, and into the small square hall. The front door was to my right, but I walked past it and over to the living room. All three rooms were the same size, thirteen feet by thirteen feet by thirteen feet. The three rooms, if you were looking at the plans for the building, or from above the building itself, formed a long space, thirty-nine by thirteen; well, slightly larger when you took into consideration the thickness of the walls, but I'm sure you'll agree with me that my figures are correct for living space. Above my little house in this block, number one of Flint Tower, there was another thirty floors, and below me there was another one hundred and nineteen. You may be asking yourself how I can remember how many floors there are to this building when I was struggling so much as to remember it was my birthday; well, let me tell you that, when you have spent years looking out the window of a room at the same view, you get to know all the little nooks and cranny's, things like how many floors a building has, which way the traffic is moving, and where the sun and the moon will be at any moment in time. Both the windows in my house faced the same way, but onto different areas. If you were to look again from above my house at the master plan, you would see the long space of three rooms, in one square room, the symbol for a window in the middle of the top wall. In the middle room, you would see the symbol for a door of the top wall, and, in the living room, you would see another symbol for another window on the top wall, so it went window, front door, window, all along the top wall of my house.

You may not think that the size of the house would be enough to actually live in. Let me tell you, the space was enough for all us people who lived in this building. There were six front doors on every floor, and one hundred and fifty floors; well, that made for a lot of front doors; too many for me to count. Even though places like this are defunct nowadays, I am going to take the time to tell you how I arrived to live here and why these towering buildings were built. As far as I am aware, these high towers were built to accommodate the less lucky people in life, the people who had come up against hard times and lost. I didn't feel like a loser, but I suppose I must have been, living here with all the other people. I had forgotten why I ended up on the one hundred and twentieth floor of Flint Tower. There was only supposed to one person living in each of the flats, hence the small, but completely liveable, space we were allowed to live in. All the buildings, this one and the ones surrounding this one, were owned by the state; that is, the state ran them for us, and, as a matter of fact, the state ran everything for us. In the morning, the state delivered our breakfast, in the afternoon, the state delivered our lunch, and, in the evening, the state delivered our main evening meal. The state also delivered our soap, razors and water. The state, every six months, arranged a meeting with each of the tenants, by means of a letter through our front door, to ask any questions we may have about our flats, and maybe solve any problems we may have inside the apartments, like, for instance, mice, a wonky door, or a broken key.

Afterwards

As I was still alive, I must have been eating, so I must have at least opened the front door to get my breakfast, usually an egg and a glass of milk, then, in the afternoon, soup and bread, and, in the evening, we had a very simple meal, a one pot dish of meat and vegetables. Very nice to eat, I have to admit, now that I think about it. If any tenant missed a six monthly appointment, usually with one of the janitors, who also lived in the building, there would be a knock at their door and, if there were no reply, the door would be off the hinges to see what the hell was going on. So you could say that the state was our best friend and, if anything ever went wrong, they would be there to help us out. If we weren't eating, they would send us to hospital and, if we weren't attending our six monthly appointments with the janitors, they would knock on the door to see how we were fairing. In some ways, now that I think about it, the state was really like the best next door neighbour you could ever have, always on the lookout for anything wrong.

So, in the living room, I made my way over to the window and opened the vertical blind. What I wanted to do was to see the moon or the sun in the sky, because I could keep perfect timekeeping just by looking at the moon or the sun. Unfortunately, it was a cloudy day, so I had to turn the radio on. As I said before, the state supplied us with everything, but the one thing we were not allowed was a television, though I never did find out why. Well, I say that there was only one thing we weren't allowed; this was not true. There were plenty of things we weren't allowed, but the biggest two things, for me, now I come to think about it, were televisions and money. The money situation, though, I understood; if we were fed, could keep ourselves clean, and were given a radio to listen to, what else could we possibly need? The basic acts of eating, sleeping and being entertained were enough for me to live on and, as I've stated before, the state was very generous, as a by-product of us having no money was that we could not get ourselves into any kind of debt. This was a blessing in disguise, because I can remember from my history books whole nations, and sometimes continents, going bankrupt because they had no money. So, once again, the state was there to help us.

The radio crackled onto my favourite station, a state-run classical music station. I liked classical music very much, and still do. I have been known to sit in front of that window for hours, and sometimes days, listening to the state-run classical music station and feeling nothing negative toward it. So, once again, I sat at the window and opened the vertical blinds so I could see the stream of cars hovering away from me and into the distance, their red lights like a highway in the sky. I waited patiently for the radio announcer to tell me the time and, as I waited, I ran my eye up and down the side of the block of flats across my from my living room window. It was exactly the same height and size as this block of flats, and housed the same amount of people as this block of flats. You could say that we were twins, these two blocks, but, in all honesty, there were thousands of these blocks of flats all over the country, all identical, all holding the same amount of people. From my living room window, I could see six blocks and, from my bedroom window, I could see seven blocks, all identical to this one, so, now that I come to think about it, we weren't really twins at all, but I didn't know the name for fourteen of the same kind of thing.

So I sat listening to some classical composer or other; I did not know who he was, but I was really waiting for the host of the show to tell me the time, as I had no clocks, or even a watch, in the flat. I couldn't remember the last time I had needed a watch, and this was the first thread of my thoughts that led me on to my last thread of thoughts of that fateful day where I made my mind up. I mean, how could you go through your life without a watch? Without time? To live without time was impossible, for, even if you did not know the time, it was still marching on around you, and it was important to know the time; well, for basic things such as when to eat, or when your birthday was.

After quite a while, the host stated that, for the last twenty or so minutes of my life, I had been listening to Beethoven, but I couldn't remember the name of the symphony or piano concerto or violin concerto that I was listening to. Eventually, he announced that it was two minutes to nine o'clock in the morning and that, indeed, it was my birth date. As it was nearly nine o'clock, I got up from my chair and went to the front door to take in my breakfast. It felt like the first time I had ever done this; I mean, to go to the front door and open it to get my breakfast; though I know that it couldn't have been. How strange a feeling to open the door knowing that breakfast was waiting for you there, but you couldn't remember doing it before. I opened the door and, indeed, there was my single egg and my glass of milk waiting for me. I looked around at the other doors I could see; all the breakfasts had been taken in, so I quickly picked up my egg and milk and closed the door for fear of meeting one of my neighbours. I don't know why I did this as I hardly ever went out, and couldn't ever remember ever speaking to anyone on the landing. It was as if I was the only person on the landing who existed, and, even though I knew all the doors had someone living behind them, it felt to me that I was the only person who existed in the world.

I boiled my egg supplied by the state and drank the whole glass of milk. I then sat at the window and began to run my eye down the side of the buildings around my building. I loved to do this and, time and time again, counted the floors of the buildings, and counted the number of lights that were burning inside the windows of the rooms up and down the tall buildings. The state only allowed anyone living in the buildings three hours of light on each bulb, so this meant, to me, that these people burning their lights were not expecting to stay up into the darkness of the night. I wasn't surprised at this, as there wasn't much to do anywhere around here. I enjoyed watching the cars fly by and imagining where they were going. All this traffic was local, as the international airways were higher and did not run anywhere near this area. I can remember the cars rolling by like a river of red light. I enjoyed this part of the day, watching the cars go by, looking up the side of the building and allowing my mind to wander through the labyrinth of time and life.

The time passed and the cars rolled by without any breaks in the traffic. I remember I felt the blood rolling around my body, and I felt dizzy. I realised I was sitting in the dark, in the silence, with no one near me, no one speaking to me, and no one thinking about me. I thought about everything I could remember, which, to be honest, was not a lot. I remember waking up this morning and remembering that it was my birthday, and I remember eating breakfast, and then sitting at the window. It was dark, and I wondered once again what time it was. My radio the state had supplied to me had been timed out; I got three hours of entertainment a day from the state, whether I listened or not, so now I had no way of telling what time it was. This frustrated me, and I can remember thinking that this was it, I had had enough of living, of existing, of breathing, of being, of sitting and waiting. I'd had enough of waking up and looking at the crack in the ceiling, of lying in bed all day long, of eating, of drinking, of walking around the house. I recall it was at this second that I wanted to end it, my life, and, as soon as I came to this conclusion, I felt much, much better.

Feeling much better, I went into the small box toilet and turned the light on. It flashed as white as a nuclear explosion in my eyes, and it took me a while to get hold of my senses again. I looked into the small mirror and felt like I was looking at an animal in the zoo, as this was not the way I remembered I looked. I gazed deeply into my eyes; their reflection dimly glowed back in my direction. This was the part of my face that I recognised, as I had grown my hair to my shoulders and a beard down to my chest. The grey hair, I thought, aged me terribly, and I looked much older than the fifty years I had accumulated. This was the final straw, and I can remember thinking about what to do next. After staring at my reflection for a while, I came to the conclusion that the only sensible answer was to phone the state and look for help to terminate my life. I wasn't worried about this and, in fact, realised that I would have to make the call and organise this myself, as it wasn't going to do it on its own. This was the worst part of being alone, having to do everything on your own, by yourself, and, after so many years alone, there is nothing you don't know about yourself, especially when the only interaction with the outside world is a crack crawling across the ceiling, or the traffic flying by the window, or eating, or listening to the radio, or turning on a light switch, or breathing, or thinking. My next challenge was to get myself ready to go outside, and I don't mean opening the front door to get my food. I mean the great outdoors. My clothes were quite difficult to find, all packed tightly in a big black canvas bag under the bed. It had been a while since I had the opportunity to get dressed. They hung off me as if they were made for a man twice my size, though I remember tightening the belt that was slung around the trousers so they wouldn't just slide off my legs to my ankles. I wore a huge brown jumper that went nearly down to my knees, and I had to fold up the sleeves a few times so my hands could be seen. The keys to the house were on the floor next to the front door, and I picked them up, making my way to the great outdoors. When I reached down to pick up the keys, a pain shot up my back, and I was glad I had taken the decision to end my life.

The landing was brightly lighted and silent. I shuffled along alone, counting my steps as I went. I followed the wall around, not knowing what to expect, and came to the lift doors; it's amazing what you can remember when you put your mind to it. I pushed on the button and stood like a piece of marble waiting for the doors to open. I remember that I had forgotten how long it took the lift to arrive, and I stood there for what seemed like an eternity waiting for the doors to open, and thought that things only moved slowly when you're trying to do something or when you're trying to move yourself. I could hardly wait to make the phone call to the state to inform them of my decision, and there I was waiting at the first obstacle.

Eventually, obviously, the doors opened, and I shuffled into the space, the mirror on the wall reflecting my image on the other side. I turned my back on myself and pressed the 'G' button; amazing what you remember after all these years. The doors closed and I descended the one hundred-odd floors, this being the fastest I had moved in years. At the bottom, I shuffled off looking for a telephone to make the call. I had a feeling that there was one somewhere on the bottom floor and, once again, followed the wall around, not really knowing where I was going to. But hey, I was right again, and there on the wall around the corner from the lift doors was a phone I could use. Luckily, these phones had instructions for use, or I'm not sure what I would have done. I read the instructions steadily and thoroughly. First, I was to lift the receiver and, to make any other call apart from calling the twenty-four-hour state hotline, I was to simply dial the number I wanted to speak to. To speak to the state, I simply dialled nine-eight-two-one. I did as I was instructed, and a phone somewhere in the city rang, though

I did not know where. I waited again for someone to pick the phone up at the other side. I read the instructions again to make sure I had dialled the twenty-four-hour number, and I had. Just as I had finished reading the instructions again, a girl answered the phone.

There was a great noise behind her, like a thousand people all speaking at the same time. I can remember her asking me to say my name and my state identification number. It had been so long since anyone had actually spoken to me that I held the phone in silence for a few seconds. She asked me once again to say my name and state my number. I thought for a few seconds more, and can vividly remember saying that my name was William Kenneth Ian Right, and she instantly asked me what my state identification number was for the third time. To my amazement, I rattled off the number to her perfectly: 0500 201 072. She immediately asked me to repeat the number, and I rattled it off again. She then repeated my name and address, as if I didn't know them, then asked what she could do for me. I told her that I wanted the state to help me end my life. She gasped slightly at this, and asked me to hold on for a second. I listened to some music while reading the instructions on how to use the phone again. She then informed me that I would have to go into the main state building in the centre of town to carry on with my request. I asked her where the building was, and she told me that she would post out the details and have them sent on by the janitor in charge of my landing. I asked her if this would be tomorrow, and she said yes. I thanked the young girl for her help, though, before I finished my sentence, she had already hung up on me. Or maybe I thought I thanked her instead of actually speaking; now, thinking back, this makes more sense to me. You know that way, when we sometimes think we've said something to someone and we haven't, and I'm sure that there is a way when you haven't said something to someone, but you think you have. I'm pretty sure I did one of these to that girl at the other end of the phone. I shuffled my way back to the lift doors and made my way back up to my floor. I opened my door and stepped inside the blackness. I remember trying to put the light on in the hall, but it wouldn't come on, as I must have timed it out earlier on in the day. I then tried to put the light on in the bedroom; once again, I had no light. I then tried the thirteen feet by thirteen feet living room light; once again, nothing. Then I remembered the toilet light, and pressed the switch down. The light buzzed into life and I stood there bathing like a moth under the moon. I must have stood there for quite a while, because the light suddenly went out on me, timing me out of my three hours for the day. At this, I felt my way through the darkness and into the living room, taking my chair by the light of the city, watching the cars fly by and the buildings stay perfectly still, as if they were all in a game like a thousand children playing a game of statues.

4
The State

I DON'T REMEMBER GOING TO BED IN THE DARK or falling asleep, but I must have, as I woke up in bed the following morning. I studied the crack in the ceiling and guessed it had not increased over the time I had been lying underneath it. I gauged this from how long it took my eyes to work their way down its length. It reminded me of looking at a map of South America, especially Brazil, and trying to guess how long the rivers were, which were continually draining into the ocean. It was a good game to play, and I'm pretty sure I would never have guessed how long those rivers were if I'd laid there in my bed for the next fifty years until I was one hundred years old. Of course, now, we all know that this would never happen, because of the decision I had taken yesterday to end my life.

Lying in bed being fifty years and one day old is no fun. The whole house was silent, and I can remember thinking about the length of a river in South America, the longest river in the world, though its name escapes me at the moment, when I heard the flap of my front door squeaking open. It was so quiet in the house that I could hear the envelope falling through the short space of air between the door flap and the floor. It sounded to me like a hand flopping down from a height under its own weight and gently hitting on some soft material. I waited for the gentle thud on the floor, then looked back up to the river crossing the continent in my ceiling. Eventually, though it was still early, judging by how light the room had become over the last hour or so, I got up slowly from the mattress I'd been lying on for the last thirteen years, and placed my weight onto the feet I'd been walking on for the last fifty years and a day. I shuffled out the bedroom and bent, my voice seeming to squeak as much as the door flap had. The envelope was a light brown shade, and I dawdled into the living room with it in my hand, making sure to check that all the buildings were in their place, as they should be, from my last check the night before. I tore open the seal, and a long white page unfolded in front of me. At the top of the page was a triangle, and below the triangle was a row of numbers. Under the numbers, I recognised my name, William Kenneth Ian Right, and, below my name, in a kind of jumbled way, a set of directions to the main buildings of the state. Of course, this, I understood, was where I had to go today to start the ball rolling to terminate my life.

First, though, I thought it would be a good idea to eat, and went to the front door to pick up my solitary egg and bottle of milk. I cooked my egg in the same pot every day and, while the egg was boiling for its five minutes, I would drink my bottle of milk. I remember exactly how long five minutes lasts; this is an easy sum. All you need to do to achieve this is count slowly to three hundred. For amusement, I can remember tapping my feet in time to my counting. So, on the first number, number one, I would tap my left foot and, on the second number, number two, I would tap my right foot. I would continue to do this until I reached three hundred and, amazingly, the last tap I tapped with my foot would always end on my right foot.

After eating, I thought remember thinking that I would have to check myself in the mirror before I set out to the state buildings. I turned the light on in the toilet and checked myself in the mirror. I looked the same as I had the day before; no great difference in the length of my beard and my hair, so, pulling on the same clothes I had worn to make the phone call to the state, I made my way once again outside my front door, and over to the doors where the lifts were. I can remember telling myself that it was appropriate that I was wearing the same clothes as yesterday, as it would feel rather uncomfortable actually going inside the state buildings with a different set of clothes on. I mean, how would the people inside the buildings know it was me, after all?

I gripped the letter firmly in my hand and made my way, for the first time in I don't know how long, outside the front door of Flint Tower. I vividly remember the weather hitting my face; the wind, I think, brushed against my skin, touching me like a lover I had forgotten existed. This made me quite afraid, and I stood perfectly still against the wind, allowing it to rub against me. While I was standing there in the wind, I was looking up at the building across the street. I had to strain my neck to see to the top of it, as it was so high and, even though I knew the walls were straight, the building looked slightly bent to me, from this angle at the bottom of Flint Tower. Once again, this frightened me, and I stood even stiffer against the weather, and now, the buildings, which I knew to be true and straight, from here, looked more bent and crooked. I counted the floors and the windows with lights on; this in itself reassured me and, after a while, the clouds rolled away from above them, and this made the buildings look as erect as I knew them to be. I recall it took a little while, but, with the sun shining and the cold weather and the buildings now erect, I remember it gave me great heart to go about my business for the day, and I gently moved forward from my spot in front of the front door of Flint Tower.

I remember that I drifted around the city feeling proud, like my own doppelganger. I spent hours watching the traffic moving over my head, looking at the underside of the cars, as though it was the first time I had even seen that. I floated through the Christmas markets like a ghost tasting the smells of Europe as I went on my way, invisible to those around me. I remember making my way to the exact centre of the city, to the square, where I sat and watched the people go by, absolutely unconnected from me here. I felt nothing for them, watching them run and walk and talk and eat and carry bags and laugh and chase and smile and drink and sit and look and breathe and stand. Everyone going somewhere I wasn't, but I knew, eventually, they would all go to the same place as me. With their hearts beating in their chests, all they were doing was delaying the inevitable or, even worse, ignoring that death was all around them, even on this day, two days after Christmas day. This, I recall, made me feel better, and I realised that I couldn't float anymore; probably something to do with the reality check of death I had just had.

Having no idea how to get to the state building, I wandered once again through the mist of the winter's day, the sun climbing high above the clouds, trying in vain to burn a hole through the wispy vapours. Quite by accident, I came across a symbol I recognised, and knew instantly that this was the place I had to go to. I will always remember the feeling that this was meant to be by me accidentally stumbling across the building. I confirmed this by looking at the diagram of the shape on the piece of paper I had in my right hand, holding it up to the triangle that was embedded on the grass in front of the building. Even though one of the triangles was made of paper and one made of metal, I knew they meant the same thing, and walked over the lawn, my shoes getting wet on the dewy grass, then made my way up the stairs to the front door of the state building.

I remember walking through the building's doors and into a huge marble hall; it looked like a building a god may stay in, with high ceilings, like sixty feet high, and marble walls and floors moving upwards away from me and vertically away from me simultaneously. There wasn't another soul in this huge building, so I decided to walk around to find someone to direct me to my meeting. Luckily for me, a man sat way down at the other end of the cavernous hall, and I shuffled towards him. He was wearing a hat like a policeman, and a blue uniform like a policeman, and I can remember asking him if he worked for the police. He replied 'no', and asked what my business was in this building. I handed the letter to him with all the information. He told me to take the lift to the second floor, go to the right, knock on the door, and wait. I did exactly as he had told me to, and found myself waiting at the door reading the instructions in case of fire, which were stuck to the front of a glass panel at the top of the door. I could not see into the room beyond, as the glass had a design scratched upon it, and I waited patiently, allowing the person on the other side of the door to open it so I could enter.

Eventually, a young girl opened the door and let me into another huge carnivorous hall. She quickly walked in front of me, sat behind a huge wooden desk, and looked straight at me. She asked me my name, and I told her, and she replied that they had been expecting me and that I was two hours late. I can remember apologising for this and stating that I did not have any way of telling the time, as I had no watch, so the only way I could tell the time was by the person on the state radio station announcing the time every half an hour. She held her hand to her nose and told me where to go. I arrived at door sixty-six and knocked gently. A man's voice from beyond the door told me to enter the room, and I can remember turning that golden round door handle in my hand as if it was yesterday, and walking over the threshold of that doorway. It felt like bliss.

The man sat in a chair behind a huge wooden desk. I can remember that the room had no windows and, as I walked over to the desk, the man breathed heavily in his chair and held his fingers over his nose, though I have, to this day, no idea why. I sat in a very comfortable chair, and he introduced himself as Mr. David Stuart. In fact, I could have guessed this, as this name was written on a piece of wood at the front of his desk and, if he had asked me to guess his name, I would have guessed, if not first, second, or third time, I would have guessed Mr. David Stuart.

Mr. Stuart started the meeting by asking me how I was. I said I was fine, and he then asked me a whole series of questions about myself, though I can only remember a few of them. He asked me my name, which everyone was asking me nowadays, and then asked me my state number, which I had never forgotten from when the number was first issued to me all those years ago. It was like a little child; I mean, how could you forget that you had a child, even if that child wasn't in your mind twenty-four hours a day, seven days a week? As Mr. Stuart asked me the questions, I can remember him writing away by hand as I spoke, and he looked at me quite seriously as I gave him the answers to the questions he was asking me. I remember him asking if I lived alone; I answered 'yes', and I remember him asking if I had a family, to which I also answered 'yes', but I could not remember their names or where they lived.

Quite amazingly, he supplied me with this information and told me that, before I left the building today, I would be speaking to my mother to arrange a meeting with her tomorrow. This was something I was looking forward to, as I hadn't spoke to Mother for quite a while now; fifty years, or something like that. Mr. Stuart kept me there for quite a while and, when he had finished asking me questions, he asked if there was anything I would like to say. I remember saying that there was nothing at all I would like to say, though, to be honest with you, I don't remember if I actually spoke those words or thought them. Mr. Stuart then stamped a piece of paper and smiled at me. He stood, walked to a door, and opened it for me. I walked through, and, behind this door, there were all types of things you might see in a doctor's room; I mean everything. There were things that we all know would be there, like a table and chairs and a doctor, but there were so many things I did not know the names for.

The doctor was called Dr. Parmajurantha. I knew this because he also had, on his desk, a little plaque that sat so you could read it. He was dark skinned and dressed all in white. In a funny accent, he asked me if everything was okay, and I can remember answering that everything was not okay and that I wanted, more than anything else, to end my life. Dr. Parmajurantha looked pleased with this answer, and scribbled down on a little piece of paper.

The next day, while I was sitting at Mother's table in Mother's kitchen, I recalled why this was a happy reply for him, then realised why Dr. Parmajurantha was so pleased. I remember the doctor asking me lots of questions, but cannot specifically remember any of them, as it was so long ago. What I can vividly remember is him asking me to take off all my clothes. I must have seemed shocked under all my hair, which was covering my face, but Dr. Parmajurantha assured me that this was standard practice for anyone wishing to take their own life. The first thing that happened was that a qualified doctor had to have a qualified look at the man wishing to end his own life. The doctor showed me where to undress, and I can remember standing naked in front of the doctor; it wasn't as bad as I'd first thought it might be, and he first asked me to open my mouth and placed a little piece of material inside it, which he then placed inside a little box. He quickly examined me, ending in some kind of brain scan with a handheld machine that buzzed away beside my right eye. This little machine made me forget all about my state of nudity, and I stood there to attention, looking at the doctor go about his professional business.

Dr. Parmajurantha told me to keep perfectly still, then he picked up a little machine from his desk and held it to my earlobe. It stung a little as the two parts of the machine met inside the skin of my ear. Dr. Parmajurantha told me that this was a little device that would keep an eye on my whereabouts from now until then. Within seconds, the doctor had asked me to get dressed, and I went behind the little screen. When I got back to the doctor's table, he was still writing away on a piece of paper. I can remember asking him what he thought, and he told me that I was a little malnourished and could do with a clean up, but, apart from that, everything was fine. There was nothing to get in the way of my personal execution.

Dr. Parmajurantha thanked me, and I thanked him, and I found myself back at Mr. David Stuart's desk. Mr. Stuart looked pleased with himself, and asked me if I knew where I was. I told him that of course I knew where I was; I was here at his desk. Once again, Mr. Stuart looked pleased with me, and he then told me that I had to give the state permission to take my life; otherwise, it would be an illegal transaction. Mr. Stuart went on to explain that an official transaction was going to take place at the point of my death. What would happen would be that, at the second I died, the state would release me from any state payments owed on the rent of my flat, or any state payments owed on the food I was given, or any state payments owed on the utility bills that the state was to pay on my behalf, or any state payments owed on the pension that I was due to receive from the state at the age of seventy-five, if I lived that long. In my case, I obviously would not be living until I was seventy-five, as I was only fifty years old, so Mr. Stuart explained that the amount of money I was to receive from the state for the payment of my funeral would be one fifth of the amount of money I would be receiving from the state if I had lived to be seventy-five years old.

I was trying my hardest to work out in a pie chart for all the figures that Mr. Stuart was throwing at me, but I just could not keep up. He informed me, though, that my funeral would be taken care of, and I would be cremated with all the rights and circumstances that any other member of society could be cremated with. This made me happy, and I was quite relieved that I would not have to pay for the cremation myself. When I mentioned this to Mr. Stuart, he laughed loudly at me and assured me that people like myself who were in the habit of saving the state housing space— in my case, three rooms of thirteen by thirteen— food— in my case, an egg for breakfast, with a glass of milk and, for lunch, soup and, for dinner, a one pot meal— and also saving the state money— in my case, a pension twenty-five years from now— and all the utility bills up until the day may have died if I was not here at this desk.

I remember Mr. Stuart assured me that people like me would be treated like everyone else who had come to a later, if not more natural, way of dying. I know now that I would be saving the state four fifths of the money that they would have had to pay me if I had to live until I was seventy-five. I saw the pie chart, the four parts of the four fifths a shade of green, and the one part of the four firths plain white; it now all made sense to me.

Mr. Stuart then held in his hand a lot of paperwork, which had to be read and signed by me and, to be honest, I cannot remember reading any of the words on any of the pieces of paper that Mr. Stuart had wanted me to read, but I can remember signing at the bottom of each piece of paper, William Kenneth Ian Right, and again, William

Kenneth Ian Right, and again, William Kenneth Ian Right. I stopped at the tenth piece of paper, and Mr. Stuart told me that this was unfortunate but necessary, and that I had to sign each and every one to make the agreement between me and the state a binding one, so I remember I went on and on and on and on signing my name, William Kenneth Ian Right, again and again, until I was finished with every single piece of paper. By the end of all that signing my name, my name looked so strange on the paper that I didn't think it was actually my name I was signing at all, but a complete stranger's name.

Mr. Stuart placed all that paperwork to the side and closed a folder on his desk. He then reached into what I can only imagine was a drawer beside his leg, and pulled out another huge amount of paper; he almost looked apologetic when he placed the papers on the table. These papers, he explained, were for the undertaking and arrangement of my funeral. He held up page one and passed it over to me; on this piece of paper there were various ways of 'assisted death'. I remember thinking that it was suicide. I ticked the box next to lethal injection, as I did not really like the rest of the options, which were: gas chamber, electric chair, hanging, beheading, burning, firing squad, and asphyxiation in orbit. It was an important decision to make, and I can remember not liking even reading the other ways to die. Yes, the words 'lethal injection' leapt from the page, and I placed a little tick next to the words.

The next sheet of paper detailed the method the state would use to get rid of my body after I had passed away. There were only three options on this page: cremation, burial, and space ejection. Once again, there was only one answer for me and, once again, I can vividly remember placing a little tick next to cremation. Now, because I had picked cremation and not space ejection, I could miss out the next thirty to forty pages, which I gratefully did. The next page directly concerning me was to do with the scattering of my ashes. It was carefully explained to me by Mr. Stuart that I would be severely limiting where my ashes could be scattered, because it was a state funeral brought on by assisted death and, even though I was tired and could hardly have been less bothered, I had to go through the protocol and tick, once again, a little box. I ticked the box that read 'Communal State Area', which sounded good enough to me. Mr. Stuart looked pleased, and told me that I would not be disappointed with my decision and, now, thinking back, I cannot remember the other options for that choice.

Mr. Stuart was happy; I could see it in his face that everything was going well for me, and that there would be no problems with the state helping me with my will. I was, after all, helping them, too. Mr. Stuart leant back in his chair and clasped his hands over his stomach. He was a thin man, with nice hair combed to the side. He had on a nice smart black uniform, with a white shirt. Or was it brown? I can't remember now. What I can remember is him stating quite clearly that we had to move on, and move quickly, as I only had three more days to live from this point. I felt strange inside when he uttered the words 'three more days', but there was little, if anything, I could do about it now. I can remember him setting the agenda of the last three days of my life.

Tomorrow, I was to go see my family and, before I left the building, I was to phone Mother and tell her that I was coming to see her. The point of this meeting with my family was to explain to them that I was ending my life three days from then, and that they were to attend the moment. The day after tomorrow, I was to have a free day. I had no idea what a free day was, but Mr. Stuart told me that it would be a day where I could do anything I wanted for the twenty-four hours of that day, at the expense of the state. You see, this was a kind of reward the state would give you for ending your life early and saving them so much money and resources.

The day after the free day was what Mr. Stuart called the clear-out day. This was the day when I was to pack all of my belongings into boxes and bags, which were supplied by the state. The reason I was to do this was to make my house ready for the next occupant, as there was a worldwide waiting list of people trying to get into Flint Tower. It was explained that, at midnight on the night of my freedom day, the state would deliver all the boxes and bags, so I could be ready for what Mr. Stuart called the big day. Of course, it was a big day, the biggest day that my life would ever see. Bigger than all the birthdays, or work promotions, or births, or marriages, or Christmases, or anniversaries I could imagine all put together, as this was to be the day of my death. I sat numb with importance.

Mr. Stuart kindly gave me a piece of official paper with everything we had talked about on it and an official stamp in the shape of a triangle. Also, it had on it a list of things I had to do, or the state could not go ahead with my cremation, and I placed this piece of paper in my pocket.

I thanked Mr. Stuart for his help and left the room. I drifted on through the corridors of power, casting no shadow under the bright lights; well, I can't remember ever seeing a shadow. I passed the man on guard, and moved on slowly through the front door. A heavy mist had descended on the city, and my sense of direction was shot to pieces as I could not see more than two feet in front of me. I glided through the mist, the tall buildings looming out from hiding like huge romantic ships. Everywhere, the people were invisible to me, and I invisible to them, wandering like a phantom over the ground. I could hear the cars above and around me, but I recall not being able to see them; this did not frighten me, though, after the meeting with Mr. Stuart and what we had arranged, so I remember saying to myself that I must, from now on, enjoy all the things that life had to offer, even if they were invisible to me. This I did floating through the heavy mist, which was now more like a thick, bleached soup. I wandered and listened and looked at the sights and sounds looming toward me, everything passing me by, not touching me, nor, I think, noticing my presence. This went on for a while, though I'm not sure how long and, suddenly, I found that I had stopped walking and was looking into the window of a shop.

    Behind me, the mist acted like a curtain against the world as I tried to look at it's reflection in the glass, but all I could see was my bearded face and long grey hair and, for a few seconds, it looked like my hair and beard were becoming part of the grey curtain of life behind me, as if the universe was trying to suck me into its very being, and I can remember saying to myself, *No, not yet; I must wait until my chosen day*. Then I came back to my senses.

    It was a large window, and I looked up at the name of the store. I read it out loud for some reason, against the cover of the mist: 'BLAKE'. It looked beautiful; a copper background and, on top, as if inscribed like handwriting, the word '*BLAKE*'. I looked in through the window, having to adjust my eyes so as not to look solely at myself. All around the display there were books, huge red leather-bound books, and huge blue leather-bound books, the kind of books that had the edges of the paper dipped in gold to protect them. Around the books, there were crucifixes of all different shapes and sizes; some were wooden, some metal, and some plastic, and they sat randomly all around the leather-bound books, upon which crucifixes were stamped onto the front cover.

    There were musical CDs, and on their front were scenes of crucifixion, and I instantly thought that this would be a good way for the state to rid itself of the people who no longer wished to be alive. Could you imagine it, outside the main state building, a row of crosses and, upon them, the grateful servants of the state hanging there, slowly passing the last few seconds, minutes, hours or days of their lives. I remember thinking that I should write to the state to ask them to introduce this method of dying, but then immediately thought that it was too late, as I was due to die in the next couple of days. Maybe someone else might come up with the idea in the years to come. I just didn't have the time anymore. My last thought of that misty day was standing looking at myself in the reflection of the window, my eyes a little closed so I could see myself better, and my body mimicking the shape of the cross.

3
My Family

I REMEMBER BEING BROUGHT BACK TO MY SENSES BY a man gently tapping on my shoulder. When I opened my eyes, the first thing I saw was my reflection in the glass of the shop. The fog had lifted and, behind me, the city was moving to and fro like a giant lung. My hands were now down by my sides, and I looked inquisitively at the man. He was wearing a pink shirt and black trousers. His hair was combed back, and I asked if it had been raining. He replied 'no'. He asked if he could help me, and I shook my head. As he walked away, he went to the front door of the shop, inserted a key into a keyhole in the wall, and turned it. The shutter to the front door of the shop slowly began to pull itself up from the ground. All the time, he was looking at me as if I was an alien. I never took my eyes from his once until he turned his back on me and entered the shop.

I knew I had something to do today, and began to think of what this thing was. I allowed the time to pass slowly in my head as I thought precisely about the day ahead. To do this, I had to begin with yesterday. I remember the fog and the walk, and then the building, and then the nice man, and then the DNA sample, and then the girl at the front desk, and then leaving the building, and then this shop, and then what? What was next? I remembered standing there as I took out a piece of paper from my pocket. God knows where I got this from, as it looked like it was seven or eight years old. I read through the first line. It read: 'go see your parents'. Vaguely, like skinning a cat, I tried to think hard about where I got this from, and then I realised that it was Mr. Stuart who had given this to me yesterday. A small piece of paper, with all my instructions on it. All the while, I was watching the man with the pink shirt walk around inside the shop, moving things around and generally killing time. I felt quite sorry for him, being a tiny part of the grand scheme of things, and here was me, a respected part of the state, doing my part for the state and myself, trying so hard to end my misery.

When I knocked on the door to my parents' house, it was answered nearly immediately by my mother. The big wooden door opened, and there she was, a lot older than I remembered her. Well, it had been quite a while since I had last seen her, but I couldn't remember exactly how long. At first, she did not know who I was. I guess that was down to the long grey hair and long grey beard I had forgotten I had grown. She looked at me suspiciously at first, her little eyes like shiny black beads, and then I could see all the wrinkles in her face change direction from a frown to a smile, and she opened her arms to greet her eldest child. It felt like being touched for the first time, as it had been so long since anyone had, I thought, even glanced at me, never mind touched me with a part of their body. I have to say, it felt strange and weird, even though I knew that this was my mother, the woman who had brought me into the world fifty years and two days ago.

She invited me into the house and closed the door against the weather; it was a nice feeling to be in a home; not a house, but a home. There is a world of difference; not that I'm going to go into that now. We walked up and into

the kitchen, where I assumed my father and sister were sitting at the kitchen table. The look on their faces... Well, you would think they had seen a ghost. My father spoke my name first.
'Will', he said to me, like he was asking a question. I said nothing to Father in reply and, in the silence, he came and put his arms around me like Mother had done. My sister then called me Will, too, as if they were trying to remind me of who I really was; you know, as if you could forget who you really were. We all sat around the table, though, I can remember there were four chairs and only three of us. Very strange, as if they were expecting someone else at the table. I asked Mother if this was the case, and she said that sometimes two of their friends came around for dinner, and that's why there were four chairs laid out. This, at least, made sense to me.
My dad and mom looked the same to me, except a lot older. I mean, I can't remember how long it had been since I had last seen them. I asked my sister who she was, and she confirmed to me that she was my sister, born two years after me. She then told me that she had been married for twenty years to a man called Andrew, and that she lived not far from Mother, and that she had three children, all teenagers now and at school or college. I genuinely felt happy for all the children involved, and wished them all happy lives, and told them I hoped they'd go on and make a success of what lay ahead for them. Well, isn't that what we're supposed to say?
My sister looked like a younger version of my mother, and I, underneath this beard and hair, looked like a younger version of Father. My mother never got tired of telling me this throughout the afternoon and, as if to prove her words, she got out the old digital photo albums for us all to look at around the table. She was correct; as I looked through the photos with my family, it was, indeed, true that I looked

like Father, and my sister looked like Mother. Is it not amazing what mothers have to know to be mothers?

We sat there for a long, long time looking through the album. There were pictures of me as a tiny baby in my mother's arms in the hospital where I was born. Although it could have been any child, it was definitely my mother in the photo, and my sister and father confirmed that the child was definitely me. This was strange, as my sister is two years younger than me, and I thought a while about how she could know such a thing even before she was born. We then looked at photos of me starting school in my little grey uniform, my skin a soft pink, and my eyes full of life. In the photos of this time, my sister had appeared as a small child toddling about, and you could see the great pride in my father's and mother's eyes in these pictures when all four of us were together.

Apparently, we used to like to go camping, as there were lots of these types of photo in the albums. There was always only either Mother or Father in the photo of us camping, for some reason. My sister and I would either be sitting around the tent with Mother or Father, walking through a field of long grass, up to our knees in a gentle stream, or standing in front of a huge rock, or next to an animal of some type, a horse or cow or sheep. In one of them— I must have been around ten years old— my father and I were standing at the top of a mountain. I knew it was the top of the mountain as, behind us, you could see the other mountains all around us, but our peak was the tallest. I remember asking him where this place was, but I now forget what he told me.

Mother stood up, as this digital photo album had finished, and made some tea for us. I looked around, slightly agog at the surroundings, and a little afraid, I have to say. The tea was lovely, and I can remember having a nice big creamy bun with the tea; my first creamy bun in years.

Mother then asked me a series of questions, for some reason, which were important for her to ask at that time. I couldn't really answer them, as I found them to be a little off topic, what with all the photos and cream buns that were being passed around. I asked her if she had any more photos of me, and she said 'yes'. She returned to the table with another digital album, and we spent another hour or so flicking through photos of me going through high school, growing taller as I went, and a lot bigger than I am just now. *I must have shrunk over the years*, I thought, seeing myself when I was seventeen years old. Mother then showed me a photo of myself on my twenty-first birthday. I couldn't believe how I looked, so young and happy with my father, mother and little sister standing around me, and a whole group of other people trying to get their faces into the photo. I must have been a really popular guy when I turned twenty-one, though I just couldn't remember the occasion at all. This felt like a terrible shame at first, though, after thinking about it, I thought I wouldn't miss what I couldn't remember anyhow.

Suddenly, Mother stood and she announced a surprise for me. I couldn't believe it, and waited as she, Father and my sister disappeared into another room. When they appeared again, they turned off the light in the kitchen, and the three of them walked toward me with a massive cake, with what must have been a hundred candles on top of it, burning like a hundred lighthouses. They looked so happy carrying the cake and singing happy birthday to me. I couldn't remember the last time anyone had sung happy birthday to me, and it may sound strange, but I couldn't remember the words to that song. All of these things were just confirming to me that I had made the right decision in terminating my life. I had forgotten what my mother looked like, as it had been so long since I had last seen her and, to be honest, I barely remembered that my father and my little sister had even existed. I remember deciding that I would not tell them yet of my decision to end my life, as they looked so happy at this moment in time.

Mother put the cake in front of me on the table. I was speechless, and Mother cautioned me about setting my beard alight on the candle flames. I looked toward them for advice.

"Blow them out," my mother instructed me.

I tried to blow them all out with one breath, but I just couldn't manage, so the three of them helped me with my second breath, and we blew them all out, the smoke from the candles rising like an old Red Indian smoke signal in front of my eyes.

They sat back at the table, and Mother gave me a huge knife to cut into the cake with. I cut four slices and pictured it in my head first; four even cuts and, for once, I had a kind of a real pie chart to look at instead of imagining one inside my head. So I cut the cake into quarters and served it on paper plates Mother had laid on the table so we could all have a piece.

We sat around that table eating my birthday cake. On my slice, I had the front wheel and bonnet, and part of the windscreen of a red car. Mother had the other front wheel of the car and the other side of the bonnet. Father had the back end of the car and the back and front windows, and my sister had the part that had the chequered flag. So, the car on the front of my cake had won the race, and I felt that this would be a good time to break the news. I didn't know which way best to say it, so I just said that I had arranged with the state that they could take my life from me with my permission. When I spoke these words to Mother, she immediately turned away from me and ran from the room, and I could sense that she was crying. In a funny way, you would think that it was her life that I wanted to take in two days' time, and not my own. Aren't mothers funny? I could tell by the look on Father's face that he was astonished by this news and, by the time I had worked my eyes around to my sister, she had already left the table and was running after Mother, calling after her, leaving the rest of my birthday cake lying there on her paper plate.

Father and I were left looking at each other, and I was still munching away on the cake that Mother had brought in not two minutes earlier. He looked very serious and cross with me, and asked me if I knew what I was doing. I remembered that I had all the documentation from the state in my pocket, which had all the correct stamps and official signatures on it. Father shrugged strangely and asked me how old I was. I replied that I was fifty years old. Father told me that he was not happy with my decision, but what could he do? He hadn't seen me for years and years and years, and I was old enough to make my own decisions, and mature enough to carry them out and, if any man was an island, that man was me. I had no idea what that meant, but I agreed wholeheartedly with the first two parts of what he said.

I was certainly old enough and mature enough to do anything that I wished to do and, for me, this was the correct thing to do. Father muttered something under his breath about too much pain in the world, but I never quite caught it. Once again, I agreed with him that there was too much pain in the world, and that sometimes that pain had to be stopped by whichever means we thought fit. I thought it appropriate to end my life, and told father that I wasn't afraid or scared, and that I had nothing and nobody in the world, but the worst part about being in my father's and mother's house with my family was that I realised I had no hope left inside me. After today, I would be dead, and I was genuinely happy inside that this would be the case, and I was genuinely happy that I was going about it in the proper way through the proper channels, and with the proper people involved.

Father couldn't argue, and didn't argue with any of those words that I just said, and I suppose that was part of being what a father was, listening to and digesting what your children had to say for themselves. This was the great difference between mothers and fathers. Fathers would sit attentively listening and contributing, while mothers would run from the table, the tears, I believe, running from their eyes at the slightest hint of any kind of suicide from one of their children. In more ways than one, I was beginning to realise that I was like my father much more than I thought, and not only in looks.

Father and I sat in silence at the table. We had both finished our cake, and were looking around the table at the walls and the ceiling. I noticed a tiny crack in the ceiling of my mother's kitchen, and followed it with my eyes over and over again. It darted left and right, looking like a flash of black lightning across mother's kitchen ceiling. I watched it carefully, and imagined a huge thunderstorm somewhere in the rain forest, one of those thunderstorms at night that light up the jungle. I could vividly see the palm trees and the tall trees and the canopy of the jungle disappearing into the distance, and then a huge crack of lightning filled the black sky and electric blue lighted up the foliage in front of me, then, a millisecond later, all was black and quiet, but I could smell the heat from the flash of lightning inside me, filling me with electricity.

My train of thought was broken by Mother and my sister entering back into the kitchen, and they sat at the table, their faces and eyes bright red as if they had been crying a lot in the last few minutes. I can remember Mother trying to talk me out of taking my life early and talking to me like I was a little child. Father sat silent as Mother tried to persuade me to change my mind. I told her that I couldn't change my mind, as I had signed the papers, and the state had signed the papers, and absolutely everything was in order and, in two days, I would be dead, and that would be the end of that. I told Mother that dying was inevitable, and then I remember asking her when her death date was. She told me that this was a completely different thing, and that everyone who was born had to pick their own death date. I remember saying that I had picked my own death date, just a long time after I should have. This strictly wasn't true, as you picked your death date when you turned thirteen years old. Everyone does this, although I could not remember the exact day that I had chosen to die; I could remember that it was in the year 2120.

Mother began crying again and left the table again. I think, looking back to that day, she knew that I was right to do this, and it was just the shock of hearing the news, and not the actual news itself, which had upset her.

The time passed, though I'm not sure how long or short that time was. I came to, and can remember looking around the table at the other three people sitting there looking at me, then something caught my attention. Buzzing above them was a little black fly. I saw it first, then listened to it buzzing over their heads. It made huge looping figures of eight above them, and I watched it for a little while as it made its way a couple of feet above their heads. They seemed oblivious to the little creature, and must have wondered what the hell it was I was looking at when, suddenly, the little fly veered from its figure of eight course and came straight at me.

In a second, the insect had landed straight on my eye. It felt heavy as it tried to pull itself from my eye. I threw my head back and closed my eyes, rubbing hard, and I recall hearing my family shout at me to open my eyes and blink. That was the last thing I wanted to do, as I could feel the animal thrashing underneath my eyelid. It felt huge, the size of a marble, and I wanted it away. I rubbed and rubbed and rubbed, and could feel the tears streaming down my face. I knew that Mother was next to me advising me, but I just couldn't put her words into any coherent order, then I could feel the insect swimming around behind my eye, and I had to fight to open my eye to try to get rid of it. Mother was telling me to hold my head up towards the ceiling and to try to keep my eye open. I could feel the liquid oozing from my eye when I looked up, and felt the cold, wet trail run down the side of my cheek and down my neck. Mother then appeared in my blurry vision with a towel or something like a towel, and began to prod the corner of it into my eye, trying to get the insect stuck on the end. I could not keep my eye open, and closed it. I immediately felt the insect make its way behind my eyeball, where I assume it was gasping for air and fighting to stay alive.

I fluttered my eyelids, the scene around me becoming more visible, and I could see in my family's eyes that they were genuinely worried about this situation. I said that everything was okay and blinked a lot, trying to flush the little animal out in a stream of tears. My sister asked if I was okay and, to be honest, I was okay, but just amazed that this insect, out of everywhere else in the entire planet, managed to fly into my eye, here in my mother's kitchen as I sat around a table with my family. I mean, what are the odds of that happening?

I was trying to open my eye wider and wider, trying to get the insect out, and I could feel something strange beginning to happen to me. Either I was getting smaller, or my eyelid was getting larger; at any rate, I could feel the world around me changing ever so slightly. The top of the table began to move upward; the ceiling with the lightning crack began to move away from me. Mother, Father, and my sister began to loom down on me from above. Mother asked if I was okay, and I replied that I was, but just felt a little strange, as if everything in the kitchen was moving away from me. By this time, I was bent over with my head between my legs, sitting on my chair, and I could see my legs were slowly but surely shrinking up the legs of the chair. I looked up at Mother, and she was looking down at me, bemused— as bemused as I was looking back up at her. I can remember asking her what was wrong with me, and she replied that my skin had grown very black and that I now had a pair of lumps forming under my clothing on my back.

I took off my shirt, and Father stated that it was a pair of wings that were embryonic, jutting out from where my shoulder blades were. The world was getting larger, and everything seemed further away to me. My body was definitely shrinking. I could see my hands withering away in front of my eyes, my fingers like sand eroding into the air each time I turned them over to have a look at them. My legs had now become spindly wires dangling from the edge of my torso. On the sides of my torso, two more legs were forming like thin pieces of thread, exactly the same as those where my arms, hands, legs, and feet used to be. On my back, the wings had now formed, though they hung limp and lifeless. Instinctively, I began to pump blood through the veins in the wings, pushing hard with all my might and, at first, they were heavily laden with new blood, then they dried out, becoming almost weightless.

I was now very small and, when I tried to speak, it seemed that I couldn't, and now, as I recall, my tongue had disintegrated in my mouth. Father picked me up in his huge hands, cradling me gently. I remember straining my neck to look up at my family from the comfort of Father's hands, though now I was flexing my wings, buzzing away on his palms. Suddenly, I took off from his hand, continually and consistently shrinking with each passing second.

They were struggling to see me flying around the kitchen and, as I couldn't speak and they could hardly see me, it was mutually decided that I should return home. I don't know how I knew, but I knew, maybe by the looks on their gigantic faces, that it was time for me to return home. Mother walked over to the kitchen window and opened it against the cold night air. I aimlessly flew into the glass pane above the gap Mother had made, and concentrated wholly the second time to get through the enormous black hole. I remember flying through that gap into the black night air, exulted and free from the confines of family and gravity. I flew off thinking that tomorrow I'd need to thank Mother for being so nice to me after all these years of not seeing her, but I suppose that's what mothers are for, even though I was just guessing.

 I headed in the general direction of my apartment, though, flying, I wasn't quite sure where that was. I aimed initially for the centre of town, following the main roads, basically the way I would have walked it. Suddenly, there was an almighty barrage of fireworks from all around, at first scaring me half to death with the noise. I climbed as high as I could, using all my energy to hover as best I could to have a panoramic view of the beautiful colours exploding from all around the city. North, south, east, west; it didn't matter where I looked, all over there was an explosion of multicoloured fireworks, and then I realised this was New Year, and this was the city celebrating the dawn of a new century. I guessed that the centre of town was where the most fireworks were exploding from, and aimed for the rainbow.

 I reached the centre of town exhausted, and rested on a gigantic Christmas decoration that was lighted from within. The heat it was generating was greatly appreciated, and I clung on upside down, watching the tops of the revellers' heads below. Energised from the warmth of the decoration, I now felt hungry and buzzed down to ground level and, finding plenty of pieces of discarded food, I ate away to my heart's content until I was bursting. It was a constant struggle not to get trampled on by so many people, and I could hardly move, never mind fly, so I found a quiet spot under the towering helter skelter, and lay down and waited for my meal to digest.

I remember lying there under the helter skelter, watching the people's feet trample by on the pavement, my belly full to bursting, and feeling exhausted, when I felt the fly inside my eye begin to wriggle behind my eyeball. It was kicking violently, trying to escape the clutches of my tears, and began to heave and pull itself free. I was blinking madly, the world outside becoming like a giant strobe, and the fly inside my eye was kicking forcefully. We worked together, helping each other, and I could feel it working its way around, and then out it popped onto the front of my eyeball, and away it flew into the bright lights of the carnival.

My little fly body began to convulse severely, and I remember that the first thing to happen was for my wings to fall off, and my fingers began to form again, and my skin began to change back to its natural colour. I was growing at an enormous rate, and was filling the rather small space I was lying under. My feet and legs returned to normal, and my hands were perfectly developed. My extra set of legs had condensed back into my torso, and I was human again, though feeling gigantic and heavy after the almost weightlessness of my insect state.

I lay there in the darkness, confused and bloated, while, all around, the normal people were having the time of their lives on this New Year's night. I crawled slowly out from under the helter skelter and stood up cold and wet, my hair and beard matted against my face, and my clothes sodden and dirty. All around me, the people were watching, the mothers and fathers and children and grandmothers and grandfathers, and I have never felt so isolated, so alone, amongst the people of my kind. I watched them all watching me. They stood in a kind of circular shape around me, as if I was a part of this carnival. I can remember thinking that I was not part of this carnival; I was not part of anything, and all I wanted to do was get out of there and get out of this life.

I was happy to think these thoughts and, when one of the security people came and led me away from my audience, I knew that I was fifty percent there on my road to salvation, whatever it may hold. On the way home, I pictured a pie chart with fifty percent; that was easy; I imagined a line halfway through a circle. Although I pictured one half of the circle red and the other blue, they were equal.

2

Freedom Day

AS I SLOWLY WOKE UP, IT FELT GOOD TO BE BACK in the apartment. I knew I was there, because the crack in the ceiling welcomed me into the day like a psychopathic mouth laughing at the world. I once again followed it over its course along the ceiling, following it closely with my eyes, feeling with them, almost *being* the crack in the ceiling. It comforted me to be here lying in this bed, the same bed I'd been lying in for the last thirteen years, watching the same crack I'd been watching for I don't know how long.

In my hand, I held a piece of paper, and I unfolded it to read through it. First, it said to go to Mother's house, then it said to have a freedom day, and then it said to report to the main state building— this was to happen tomorrow. So today was my freedom day, and I wasn't sure what was going to happen. I had a plan to feel good and happy about things today, but even the best-laid plans were difficult to follow. I watched where the edge of the wall met the ceiling, and followed where they met as I done a thousand, or maybe a million, times before. I had no idea what time it was, so troubled myself to get out of bed and turn on the radio in the living room. I gently got to my feet, my back aching. God knows why it was aching, as all I had done

yesterday was visit Mother and meet my family.
 I couldn't remember leaving Mother's house and getting back to here. I toddled through the thirteen by thirteen hall. By the front door, I noticed that there was an envelope lying on the hall floor. I decided that first I would find out what time it was, then open the envelope on the hall floor. I switched on the radio, and the sound of some orchestrated piece of music came from the small speakers. I sat by the window and peeked out at the buildings across from me, quickly counting the floors from the bottom up, then from the top down. I remember the cars flying away from me and the music reaching a crescendo. I knew this was the end of the piece, and waited for the presenter to tell me the time. She told me it was eight-thirty in the morning, and I slowly stalked through the rooms to the front door to pick up the envelope lying there.
 Inside the envelope was a letter from the state and, more precisely, a man named Mr. Edenburg. He had written to me in his own hand that I was to meet him at nine o'clock this morning to begin the process of my freedom day. So, I had half an hour. I went out to the hall and opened the front door to take in my breakfast, which I knew was sitting there waiting for me. As I bent, my back aching, the door across from my front door opened. I believe that this was the first time I had ever seen that door open, and out stepped a man, about my age, grey short hair and casual clothes. He stopped and stared at me as if I was a murderer or something like that, and I stood erect, holding my milk and egg. We both stopped and said nothing, though, underneath my beard and hair, I was trying to speak to him. I wanted to speak to him and tell him what was happening to me today, but I just couldn't face opening my mouth and talking directly to this man I had just met.
 I remember that he told me he had just moved in next

door, and that, in fact, this was the first time he had left his new apartment. I just stared at him. He asked me if the block was okay to live in and, once again, I can remember just gawping at him through my hair. He took a step toward me, with his hand outstretched, and told me his name was David. Or was it Stephen? I can't remember now. I looked at him with my egg in one hand and my milk in the other, and it was as if he kind of woke up and grunted something low under his breath, then walked away. I stared at the spot he had walked from, not watching where he went; I mean, I just stood there running my eyes up and down the shape of his front door, around its edges, until I was satisfied. This was the first time I had ever looked at that door, and I could have stood there all day, but then I remembered that I had to go meet someone from the state to have my day of freedom. Whatever that was.

I knew it took five minutes to boil my egg and, as the bubbles in the water began to form, I dropped in the little embryo and began to count out loud to three hundred, tapping my feet as I counted. Two hundred and ninety-nine, then three hundred, and I poured the water from the pot, emptying it all into the sink. The egg was hot and hard, and I devoured it, cooling off its heat with the coolness of the milk. This was the best breakfast anyone could have, as I don't ever remember having any other kind of breakfast.

I picked the pieces of egg from my beard as I began to change from my night clothes to my day clothes, as recently, I had been busy going here and doing this and talking to whomever, and I thought it was always better to do these things not naked. So, over the past few days, or weeks, perhaps, I had got into the habit of changing my clothes at night before bed, then again in the morning when I woke up when I had to go out. It was a terrible nuisance for me to remember to do this, but I knew I must do it to make all the things in this week go well and true.

I was ready, and walked through the darkness of the hall, watching the little lights peeking through the keyholes like stars in the night sky. The light flooded in when I opened the door, as if there had been a spectacular explosion somewhere in the night sky. Stepping out onto the landing, I closed the door behind me, and a huge shadow fluttered by me. I stopped dead in my tracks, confused and thinking. I slowly looked around the space in front of me, and couldn't see a thing, so I imagined that I had imagined the shadow. Then I felt a buzzing around my ears, and a tiny gust of wind floated by me. My eyes caught up with the figure floating around in front of me. I remember seeing a bird, a robin, scurrying around in the air, and I think the little bird was confused and lost, because I don't think a place like this is where birds like to stay and, even if they did like to stay in spaces like this with no sunshine and no food, this bird was very unhappy at living in a space like this.

I walked by the bird and wanted so much to leave it in here and go about my business on my freedom day, but I just couldn't press the button to summon the lift. I could hear the little bird's wings beating against the air, and it sounded to me like a humming bird, but I knew it couldn't be a humming bird, as they don't even live outside in this country, never mind inside. I watched it tumble and crash into the walls, excited. I toddled over to the thing, watching it going crazy in this confined space.

I waited and waited, although I don't remember how long I waited, as I couldn't see outside to see the sun or the moon. I waited until the little thing was exhausted, and then, slowly, I bent an inch at a time, so as not to frighten it further, then, suddenly, I clasped the bird in my hand, applying the exact amount of pressure so as not to kill the little thing. Strangely, this reminded me of God and all the bad work he had done for me. I couldn't remember exactly everything that God had failed me in, but I can remember thinking that, if I was the bird and I was resting in God's almighty hands, God would apply the wrong amount of pressure and squeeze and squeeze and squeeze me until He had crushed the very life from me. But not me, no. I wasn't God.

Holding the little bird in my hands, I pressed for the lift with my knuckle and waited. I could see the little beak and all the goodness of its feathers between my fingers. As the lift door opened, I stepped through the light, and the bird twitched inside my temporary finger cage. It was a long way down, and I can't remember ever meeting anyone at all in the lift, except on this day when, obviously, I had so many other things to do, and then I met this woman, or it might have been a girl, who got on halfway between my floor and the ground floor. She entered the lift space and stared bewilderingly at the bird. Or was it at me? I can't remember, but she looked astonished.

The three of us said nothing as we descended. The girl's— or woman's— eyes were wandering all over the tiny space we now existed in, and I could feel her fear and that she wanted to ask either me or the bird a question. I can remember the door opening when we got to the bottom, and it not only let us leave the lift, but let all the tension out, too, and, at last, I could breathe again. The girl walked in front of me, and I can remember shouting at her to hold the front door open for me as my hands were full with the robin. She did this for me, and watched as I opened my hands, letting the bird go, but it did not fly away; it sat on my hands with its legs hanging over the edge of my fingers and its body resting on my palm. I watched the robin, the robin watched me, and the girl watched us both, her blue eyes flitting between us.

Suddenly, the bird loped forward and, within a millisecond, was standing proud on a fence over the street.

The girl immediately let the door go, and we both walked toward the bird, which looked so proud and elegant with its little red breast puffed up like a tiny balloon. It darted away again, out of sight, and the girl and I looked at each other.

From behind me came a voice calling my name, and I looked around trying to think of anyone who knew my name around here. Then I realised that the state had arranged my freedom day for today, which was the initial reason I had left my house today, and not, as it may seem, to free the robin trapped inside the building. I turned to see the girl one more time, but she had gone, too, leaving me on my own to talk with another two people I didn't know.

The man who had called my name introduced himself as Mr. Edenburg; a strange name, I know, but that was his name. He spoke in great detail to me about this day and how important it was for me and the state that I used this time wisely. I can remember him saying that today would be the last day I would not have any responsibilities, and that I was to use the twenty-four hours, or, in my case, the fourteen hours I had left, so that I wouldn't have any regrets. I told Mr. Edenburg as I was getting into the car that I wasn't sure about what it was I had to do today, as I had never had a freedom day.

Mr. Edenburg told me that this was a common thing among people like me and, as he closed the car door behind him, he tapped the shoulder of the man in the front of the car and asked him for a schedule. He took the schedule from the man in front, then the engine was turned on. I could feel the car's engine ticking away behind me, and I remember asking Mr. Edenburg if this was a flying car. Mr. Edenburg told me that it was, and I told him I had never flown before and that this could be the first thing on my list on my freedom day. Mr. Edenburg looked happy at this, and smiled at me as we lifted off the ground. There were lots of lights in the front of the car displaying messages to the driver, and I couldn't remember if I had ever been in a car before, although I remembered that I had definitely never been in a flying car before.

So, we first joined the traffic at the low-level local height, and then, at the junction some ten minutes later, we joined the traffic at the national height. I watched the city moving by us, and watched the buildings' edges as they slid up between the streets, pointing at the sky. It was great to see new buildings and watch them drift by at a much faster pace than walking. There were tall buildings, short buildings, and long buildings; in fact, there were buildings of all shapes and sizes. I never took my gaze from the window and, even though I remember feeling a little sickly, it was still very exciting.

Mr. Edenburg asked if I would like to fly higher in the car. I answered 'yes', and we flew for another fifteen minutes until the next sky junction, which was for international travel. The ground looked as if I was looking at a map of the world in a book. I could see fields and rivers and oceans from where I was sitting in the back of this car. Mr. Edenburg then asked if I would like to go into space. I didn't know what to say, but I guess from the look on my face he guessed that it was a yes.

We flew at the same height for quite a while, the driver obviously knowing where to go all the time. Then we began to climb as the driver spoke to someone, somewhere, on his headphones. We climbed and climbed and, as we climbed, the air in the car began to hiss. I must have looked worried, as Mr. Edenburg immediately told me that the air was escaping because the car had to be airtight, or we may be sucked into space or, even worse, frozen to death. As the air escaped, the Earth grew smaller below my feet, and then the noise stopped from inside the car and the engine also cut off. Mr. Edenburg told me to fasten my seatbelt, which I did, and Mr. Edenburg and the driver did the same.

Soon afterwards, I remember watching the way the Earth curved around like a giant ball in space, and then the schedule on Mr. Edenburg's leg began to float, and I remembered that there was no gravity in space, nothing to pull us towards the centre of the Earth, as we were free from its spinning surface. I can remember sitting there with Mr. Edenburg, and the driver flying around the very edges of the planet we call Earth, feeling like a giant, feeling like I knew everything was going to be okay, and feeling like the state was a good thing and that it was looking after me. I mean, after all, this was space I was in.

The Earth 'tumbled around', and we flew around the Earth, everything moving, nothing stagnant. I could see the sun shining far away in the distance, beaming, radiating, at the centre of everything. I watched it as we moved between the orbs, the big yellow star staying perfectly still no matter how close or far away we went, the vast distance between us making all the difference. I remember thinking that this was a bit like death, the space between the living and the dying, so vast, as if it didn't matter, as if we didn't matter. This made me realise that I had made the right decision about my death in one day's time, and I felt good. I watched the sun, and it watched me back, as it had been watching back for billions of years. I wanted to go back to Earth now, and we slowly made our way back toward the pull of the big ball.

Back in the Earth's atmosphere, Mr. Edenburg handed me the schedule. I opened the pages and flicked through the brochure; there was nothing really that I could have said I wanted to do. There were events like sporting games and concerts, and all kinds of different things, but I didn't really want to go somewhere with lots of other people. I said this to Mr. Edenburg, and he asked if I would like to be alone for a while with my thoughts. This, for me, was a good idea, and I said 'yes' to that. Then he asked me where I would like to go to be alone with my thoughts. I kind of shrugged and told him that I wasn't sure of a good spot to be alone. Mr. Edenburg smiled and tapped the driver on the shoulder, and, without saying anything, the driver turned the car north, heading to an isolated spot.

We must have been flying for a while, and I didn't recognise where we were, but it was beautiful. The doors to the car opened, and the wind howled inside, gnawing us to the bone. Mr. Edinburg got out the car and walked away. I followed closely, while the driver stayed in his seat. We were walking over thick, deep, short grass up a steep hill. I say walking, but I was more stumbling, trying to get up the hill. Mr. Edenburg held my arm and guided me up towards the place of isolation. He was telling me that, when he felt low or depressed or just needed some time on his own, he would come up here to think and, as it was my freedom day, and tomorrow I was going to die, he thought it would be a good idea if I shared this spot with him.

We got to the top of the hill, and I turned back to look for the car. Amongst the green of the hills, it was a small black dot sitting in the distance. We rounded the top of the hill, the wind blowing my beard and hair nearly straight out behind me. My hands were cold, there were tears running down my face, my nose was running, and I was beginning to wonder where we were going when, suddenly, in front of us loomed a cave. We walked like missiles, cutting through the air, and entered the cool, dark recess.

Mr. Edenburg lighted a fire with the remnants of his last visit, and I watched the yellow flames dance in my mind like a hypnotist's suggestion. Mr. Edenburg asked if I was okay, and I stated that I was. He told me that, in one hour, he would return, and that I was to use the time well. I sat behind the fire, looking out at the rolling hills in front of the cave. Mr. Edenburg disappeared from view and left me alone with the flames. I held my hand out to warm them against the blustery winds, and now the only sounds near me were the sounds of the wind and the fire, and the voice in my head, which I feel had been talking to me nonstop throughout my life.

I wanted it to stop, as it brought so much pain, reminding me and trying to remind me of things that I would rather not remember. I sat in the dark, the flames throwing a huge shadow on the cave wall behind me, the light from the sun bundling through the clouds in a milky residue, the grass rolling away from me, undulating like the waves on the open ocean, and meeting the sky somewhere out there in the distance. Looking down at the flames, I let my mind wander, though it didn't get far, back to the apartment and the flats across the street, light bulbs, the crack on the ceiling, the cars in the sky, and then I remember that random thought leading me somewhere I had deliberately forgotten, her face, happy, holding my daughter in her arms, the photograph now lost. We were so old fashioned that morning, the two of them inside the car, driving away from the house never to return, my daughter waving from the back window of the car as it pulled out the driveway.

Strangely enough, I got a feeling so weird that day that I thought I was coming down with something, but no, it was God telling me that I was never going to see my family again, telling me in the way God knows how, by a feeling in the pit of your stomach. What I would do now to never have felt like that on that fateful morning. I remember going about my business on the day, kind of worrying slightly about my wife and daughter, who's names I can't quite remember at this moment in time, and then I got a message from my parents-in-law asking me to make my way to their house, which I did as soon as I could, and I remember arriving at their house, and they were there with the police, and I knew, even before they told me, and they said that the crash was so bad that the bodies were burnt beyond all recognition, and that they would not be able to be identified because of the severity of the accident and the amount of bodies involved.

Apparently, people get moved about in large automobile accidents, even if they were well strapped in when they crashed. I remember that there were forty other vehicles involved in that accident, buses, oil tankers, cars, and lorries; they all seemed to be there at the wrong time and, even though no one knows how the crash began, they know that over ninety people were killed in the pile up, the vehicles a mangled wreck like metal spaghetti. I remember it was reported in one newspaper that the fire after the collisions reminded onlookers of what the fires of Hell may look like. So my wife and daughter were burnt to death, trapped in their car amongst the metal and the bodies and the flames, and I remember trying to forget this accident lying in bed crying, trying not to remember, and trying not to feel that last few horrific moments of their life. I'm okay about it now, but then, it was the beginning of the end of me.

Yes, yes, I'm okay; thanks for asking.

I came to in that cave watching the flames lick around my hands like a tamed wild animal, and I watched out from the front of the cave, the darkness slowly descending on the wilds of the countryside, and I felt that wind blow around me and through me, and I thought about the thousands of years that humanity had been on the planet, and how insular we all were, and how anti-nature we had become. Everything was for us— the state, the cars, the houses— everything we saw was for humanity, and I can remember thinking that I wasn't part of humanity, and that I couldn't wait to be dead and be out of the clutches of the randomness of God's will, and I cursed God until Mr. Edenburg came back to the cave, the fire now burnt out and me sitting there in the darkness, the tears rolling down the hair on my beard.

For the first time in I don't know how long. Now, thinking back, I'm sure it was the return to nature that made me remember my late family, the simple things; it is crazy how the mind works when we let it roam, and that was, in some way, a blessing for me to go on from that day and carry out my voluntary death. It felt good to be there for the last and first time, exploding with emotion at the death of my family, knowing fine well that the last chapter of us was to be finished tomorrow. I remember thanking Mr. Edenburg for the use of his cave. He said nothing to me, but led me once again by the arm over the crest of the hill, back to the car, where we took off into the setting sun through the gale force winds and the pelting rain. I was relieved to be leaving the countryside and to be heading back to the city.

We landed back at Flint Tower, and I remember that I was never so happy to see the walls of the block stretching high up into the sky. As we sat in the back of the car, Mr. Edenburg said that he would see me tomorrow at some point, and that the driver would be here for me if I needed any help for anything at all. He also explained that I could go anywhere on foot, but had to be back in my apartment before midnight. I didn't question this, and entered the building, feeling relieved to be back in the apartment.

The rest of that day is ever so vague to me now, but I remember a dream or an event that I was sitting there in the dark of a park. The grass was black where the moonlight didn't manage to shine. I sat there alone, watching the small pond in front of me not move. If it had been a square shape, the pond would have been thirteen feet by thirteen feet square; as it was, it was a round shape, but I don't know how to round things off mathematically. It was a mirror reflecting the light from the stars, the darkness of the sky, the light from the buildings, the shadows from the trees, and the coldness of the air.

In that pond, there existed the universe, and I so much wanted to touch the universe before I died. I can remember how cold it was as I took off my shoes and socks and rolled up my trousers, and then I dipped my feet into the pond of the universe. Instantly, I lost control of my bladder, felt the hot urine run down my leg, and saw it darken the fabric of my trousers. I watched that ripple move across the surface of the pond from the disturbance of my feet. At first, nothing happened as the ripple only moved across the dark side of the pond, which reflected nothing visible back into the universe, then I watched as the reflection of the moon was chopped into a multidimensional monster by the ripples across the surface of this tiny universe.

I was watching the moon in the pond, and then the moon in the sky and the edge of the pond, and then my mind began to wander and think about circles. I was watching the edge of the full moon, following it around, and then I was thinking about the edge of the Earth, all round, and then I began to think about the edge of the pond, a perfect circle, and then I began to think about cycles, like the cycles of weather and the cycles of bodily movements and the cycles of life and death and the cycles of sleeping and the cycles of going to work, and then I began thinking about the way things have worked and worked and worked over the last billions of years, and this made me feel good about tomorrow, and all this infinite stuff made me feel like I was going to be part of the universe at last, and not be a blight on the surface of humanity, but be a floating organism within the fibres of the invisible all around us, like a molecule of hydrogen.

The surface of the pond began to even out as my feet were at rest in the water. The water clung to my shins, and I could nearly feel it pull me under with its gravity, but then

I thought, *No, I must wait for tomorrow and do it properly*. The ripples on the surface of this tiny universe had stopped, and I watched the reflection of the moon gently weave about and bend and stretch like molten silver in a crucible, until all became calm. There was no noise; well, none I can remember. I sat there for a while— I don't know how long— looking at the reflection of the universe in the tiny pond, and feeling glad that I was physically a part of it and that, tomorrow, I would be consumed by it and be turned to ether within the flames of the crematorium.

Looking at the moon, I can remember thinking that I had to get back to the apartment before midnight. I don't know why, but this was a clear instruction in my agenda for this freedom day. I lifted my feet from the infinite pool once again, causing mayhem on its surface, annihilating the lunar surface reflected and now not visible through the turmoil. I walked through the black grass, my shoes and socks in hand, and my feet freezing to the bone, and, not only my feet, but the urine stain on my trouser leg had also begun to freeze, and I limped slowly like a wounded animal back through the light from the stars and the cars in the sky, all the way back to Flint Tower.

1

My Final Day

I REMEMBER WAKING UP ON THE BED AND WATCHING that poor crack in the ceiling, feeling its way away from me. In a couple of days, there would be someone else lying here watching the crack in the ceiling, though I doubt very much if that crack in the ceiling would give the other person any genuine happiness at all. I don't think the crack on the ceiling would give any other soul an ounce of pleasure, as I think me and that crack had it coming; it was our fate to meet and get to know one another, and for it now and again to inspire me and carry me away. I doubt very much if this would ever occur again in this room.

I dressed simply for the day, basically covering my nakedness and, even though there was no one around, I felt that this would be the proper thing to do, as this was the final day I would be alive. I sauntered into the living room and peeked through the window at the blocks of buildings across the way from me. It was reassuring to know that they were still there, and I counted all the floors from top to bottom and from bottom to top by moving my eyes steadily over them. The cars in the sky continued to flow by, all their red lights like little devil's eyes staring back at me. This took a while, though I don't know how exactly long, and I was kind of woken from my meditation by a rather loud knock on the front door. I brought myself around to the sound and toddled off to answer it. When I opened the door, allowing the artificial light to come streaming across my hallway, there stood the driver from yesterday who had taken me into space and back, in the back of his car. He told me that he was to be my guide for the last day, and that, if there was anything I specifically wanted, I was to tell him immediately; after all, I was going to die today.

My guide told me that I had an agenda for today, and that I had to meet all the things on my agenda so as not to cause any waves, or even ripples, for the events that were to happen. First, I was to wash all my clothes, then I was to clean the apartment, then I was to label everything I didn't want the next tenant to have. I nodded and knew that this would not take me long. My guide from the state handed me a roll of labels and a pen, and told me he would be back later on to check that I had carried out these simple tasks. The light from the hall narrowed to a slither as I closed the door on him, leaving me in the darkness again.

I remember labelling the bed right away, as I felt that this bed was mine and, after thirteen years of sleeping in it, no one else was ever going to have the pleasure. I thought about labelling the crack in the ceiling, but decided not to. Well, for one reason: I couldn't reach up to it to stick the label to it. There wasn't much else to label. I felt that it would be nice to leave the table and chair in the living room so the next person could sit and watch the days go by, so I did not label the table and chair. In the kitchen, I only had a small pot and some odds and ends of cutlery, so I did not label them, either.

That was that; there was nothing else, so I gathered the clothes I did not have on, and set about going upstairs to the laundry room at the top of Flint Tower. It had been a long, long time since I had been up there, for no other reason than actually making the effort to go up there. My clothes were heavy inside the bag, and I could only drag them to the lift door and, this time, instead of pressing 'G', I pressed 'L', and, for the first time in God knows how long, the cable turned the other way for me and carried me upwards toward the laundry floor.

The lift doors opened, and there stood a huge room on one floor, full of laundry equipment; something else to thank the state for. I dragged that bag behind me to the nearest machine and, placing my clothes into the washing machine, I was trying to imagine how I would feel later on in the day when I was about to die. Having never died before, I struggled to think what was going to happen to me. I had picked my method of dying: by injection. For me, this felt like a more humane way to pass on. It meant that my body would be intact, even though all my body parts would be used again after I had stopped breathing. This wasn't a problem for me; I didn't mind the fact that I would be being used by another person in the world. In fact, I found this quite amusing. I can remember thinking about what it would feel like for someone else to be looking out of my eyes at all the things they would see in their life. Their family, their holidays, the sunsets and the all the girls, and then I thought, *What if it is a woman who gets my eyes?*

Did they do that? Did the state give male eyes to females? In the end, I suppose it didn't matter too much, because eyes were just eyes, just the same as hands were hands and feet were feet. Even though I had become attached to them, it was wise to think of all the sums of my whole, so to speak, being in fact, not me, for, after tomorrow, I would not exist, but the various parts of my body would.

This was too much for me to think about, today of all days, so I sat there watching the washing machine move around in its cycle. First, it filled with water and spun around a little to wet the clothes, then it added the soap and spun around a little more. Little dots of soap appeared on the round window at the front, and the machine began, in earnest, getting rid of the dirt from my clothes. I watched it like someone may watch an entertaining show on the television; it certainly allowed me to pass away half an hour of my life.

My mind was wandering from here to there, and I felt safe in the knowledge that, later today, everything would be taken care of; for the first time in my life, I wouldn't have a thing to worry about. Not about shaving, or washing, or getting a job, or getting married, or getting out the building I lived in, trying to get up the ladder of success. These were all things that basically took your mind off what life was about: living. I never really understood all that stuff until that moment in the launderette at the top of the building and, when I took my clothes out of the machine, they felt damp and alive, for I knew that the day after tomorrow someone, somewhere, would be wearing them to keep themselves warm on the first day of January 2100.

It then suddenly dawned on me that this was the first day of a New Year. Where the hell had it gone? Today was the first of January 2100. *Quite a milestone for the world*, I thought. I can remember thinking about the world on its axis, spinning around, and of our little human years slipping by like raindrops in a thunderstorm or musical notes written for a symphony, and that the Earth didn't care if we were here or not, because the Earth was here and, without the Earth, we would be nowhere. There was one difference between us and the Earth: the Earth couldn't think for itself; it couldn't think, but it could fight and, if the Earth began to fight the humans, we would all be doomed.

Then I thought that the Earth had been around for billions of our years, and would be around for billions of our years after we had all passed on, and that we live for so long on this planet and it doesn't matter what we do or what we say or what happens to us, because this planet beats us all when it comes to everlasting life and we… Well, we are so coincidental, like a grain of salt amid the billions and billions and billions of grains of salt there were inside this planet. This thought made me feel good, to be here on the first day of January 2100, and to know that later, on the second of January 2100, I would not be here; I would be there, wherever there was.

The time passed quickly for me between certain parts of the day, and the next thing I remember is my door being knocked again. My door had never been knocked so many times as it had done in the last week, although it did make me feel important to have so many people from the state checking up on me so often. I wandered through the rooms before answering the door, making sure the label was still stuck to the bed and that my clothes were still all bagged at the front door. I let the man from the state in, and he walked around the apartment looking at all the things that I had just looked at; this, I thought, was a waste of our time, but he did it anyway.

After this, the day drifted by. My guide from the state was very quiet in going about his business. This didn't bother me at all, as I was used to no noise from the inside of my apartment, apart from the noise of the radio every now and again. Suddenly, the guide spoke and told me now was that time. Surprised, I asked, "What, now?"

He nodded. For a second, I stopped breathing, and it felt like I had hit a wall or something as hard as a wall. Everything stopped suddenly. My thoughts stopped, the world stopped, the lights stopped shining, the air stopped moving, and all life stopped existing. Of course, I know now this was all in my mind, like everything else I had carried around with me for my fifty years, and then everything began to move again, but it moved like it was out of tune, as if the laws that guided us through our lives did not exist and I was moving independently from the rest of you out there. I took the first step on the road to my lat step, and closed the door on the apartment.

On the way down to the car with the guide, I couldn't help but try to think of what had got me into this position, and how it was that I had managed to be here now. I couldn't remember anything about it. I could remember being at the launderette this morning, and going in the car and flying into space and walking through the mist and floating down the Amazon, but I could not remember how I had managed to get myself here today with this guide from the state walking me to his car, taking me to a place I didn't know the location of. I decided to stay calm, and sat in the back of the car. We took off through the air and, within minutes, we were at the roof of the building where I was to meet Dr. Edenburg again.

I was taken from the car by the guide, and three other men greeted us, though they did not speak. The five of us went over to the door on the building's roof and descended the staircase to the first floor, which was, ironically, the last floor; it all depended which way you were coming from. The five of us entered a room, where a young girl seated at a desk asked me my name. I told her my name was William Kenneth Ian Right, and I can remember that she smiled at me as if she was really pleased to hear my name, for some reason. She waved, and it led my line of vision to a large set of double doors. I looked at her, and she at me, and I knew that I had to go through those doors.

I nearly laughed when I saw what was through those large double doors. There was a long, long row of showers away at the back of a long, long room and, before those showers, was a wall covered with mirrors from floor to ceiling. At the end of the room with the showers, there was steam drifting just under the ceiling like a large, wet cloud. My guide from the state invited me to walk by the mirrors. Placed in front of the mirrors were a few chairs, which looked comfortable to sit on. I watched myself drift past those mirrors effortlessly, not taking my eyes from my own reflected eyes as I walked toward the showers. For the second time this week, I was asked to take off my clothes and, by now, I thought I had grown quite accustomed to this stripping off. I did what was instructed, and I was then invited to walk through the showers and wash. I remember the shock of the hot water as it hit my body, the little drops of warm water feeling like daggers against my skin. Soon, though, I was under those shower heads like a baby in a bath and washing myself over and over again to get clean.

The guide from the state put a stop to this, though, and walked into the steam to retrieve me from my fun. He told me to get ready by putting on a huge white dressing gown. I was then ushered over to one of the chairs in front of the huge, mirrored wall, where a man appeared as if from nowhere and began to shave off my hair. I didn't know what to say or do, so I said and did nothing. He then proceeded to shave off my beard, first cutting with scissors, and then getting in close with a razor, and I could feel the weight falling off my head during this grooming. I couldn't see a thing, as the mirrors were all steamed up from the showers and, at the end of this haircut, I was again asked to go shower.

Under the water, my face felt very smooth and awkward to touch, and my head felt burning hot from the water hitting my scalp directly. I washed and washed and washed myself, over and over again, as if I was never going to have the pleasure of this again. Suddenly, the water was turned off and I took the hint to get myself dried and ready for the rest of the today. I stepped out from the shower area and dried my head; it was really easy compared to having to dry all that matted hair, and I was dry in seconds, rather than hours. There was a set of clothes set out for me, and I put them on.

I was then instructed by my guide to sit and wait for a few minutes until Mr. Edenburg was ready to see me. I never thought for a second that Mr. Edenburg would be there, and this pleased me. The windows of the room were opened as I sat and stared at the ceiling, watching the clouds of steam evaporate into nowhere. My guide motioned me toward the door, and I walked past those mirrors, wondering who the hell it was reflected in them. The skin on my face was flushed pink. My hair sat tightly against my head, showing off my cheeks and ears. I couldn't honestly remember the last time I had seen any features on my face, although I couldn't remember ever looking as distinguished as I did with my short hair, shaven face, and black, pressed clothes. It felt good to be like this, and I couldn't wait to thank Mr. Edenburg for all the attention to detail he had obviously put himself through to get me this far through the day.

I was led down the white-washed corridor to a little room with a small table, and a chair beside it. On the table lay a blue, leather-bound book, like the one I had seen in the shop a couple of days ago. This reminded me to tell someone about crucifixion as a way to end your own life, and then I immediately thought that it would take someone more than me to bring this idea forward to the likes of the state. I sat and ran my eye around the shape of the cross on the cover of the book, then around the edges of the book, then I naturally followed, from a line I had drawn, from the book to the edge of the table, and I followed the setting of the table here in this room, and then ran my eye up the wall and around the room, where the ceiling met the walls.

There were no cracks in the ceiling of this room, and I

let my eyes wander around the bleakness of this space. At least, in my apartment, there was character; there were cracks that allowed the mind to flow and ebb and drift. In here, the atmosphere was sterile. I was moving my eyes around the room where the wall met the floor, following it around in a square shape, and thinking and wondering what was going to happen next when, immediately, the door opened and in came a man I had never met before. He was dressed in white, and asked if I was hungry. I nodded, and he then asked what I would like to eat. I replied that I wasn't sure, and asked him what he had to offer me. He replied that I could have anything to eat in the world. I asked him what time it was, and he told me it was nearly ten at night. I can remember asking him to get me steak and potatoes, something I'd not eaten for... Well, I don't know how long, or if I'd ever eaten steak and potatoes, but it was something I was going to try tonight.

I sat there in the bright white light, with something or other nagging away at the back of my mind. I couldn't remember what, and I just sat waiting, watching the bare walls and, where the different surfaces interacted, I played my eyes over them. I don't know how long I had been sitting when the man came back with the food I had ordered and placed it in front of me on the table with a glass of water. I remember devouring that plate of food, and can remember every single tiny sensuous piece of meat that entered my mouth, even to this day.

The man stood over me silently as I ate the meal and, when I was finished, he took the plate from me. We didn't speak at all, except when I asked to go to the bathroom, and he escorted me down the corridor further and waited outside for me to do my business. We slowly walked back to the room with the table and chair and book, and he closed the door behind me, leaving me alone. I waited and let my mind wander around inside the room and around the universe. These were the best times, being lost in the universe, being alone, feeling each second in front of you, knowing that now was the oldest and newest time, knowing that now, this second, was new, and that nothing can exist, as each second is conceived anew from the last. It is only our sense of cohesion that builds it all up into something physical, something we think we can touch, like the walls or words on the pages of a book.

I began to shiver and feel very cold at this point, a certain kind of realisation that I was going on a journey, the ultimate trip, and knowing that I was correct to do so. There was no difference in being alive or dead; the time moves on; we are only unaware of it. Then it dawned on me that I had been dead for quite some time, wandering around like a ghost, like mist, blowing here and there, and I was happy, genuinely happy, that I was going to die. I sat back in that chair and sighed heavily, glad to be escaping the clutches of the binding that this life had thrown at me. Nobody wins; nobody loses; we move through the world in the sun and the rain and the wind, in love or hate, in thought, in feeling, in everything, and then we face this: the death of everything. There was only one question left to answer: why were the cards all stacked the wrong way for me? This was something I was waiting for God to tell me.

A man dressed in white opened the door to the little room and held me gently by the arm, breaking my train of thought. He guided me down the same corridor by the toilet door and, at the next door on the left, I heard muffled voices coming from within.

Mr. Edenburg greeted me at the door to the chamber, and I can remember him saying to me that it was good to see me out of those rotten rags and looking human, or was it humane? I can't quite remember. I peeped inside the room while he was speaking to me. The room was all in white; the chair, the instruments, the walls, and all the people were all in white, too, from their masks to their hair nets, to their white overalls and white rubber boots. Amazingly, there was a clock on the wall, and I couldn't take my eyes from it. I watched the second hand flick, one movement at a time, around the three hundred and sixty degrees back to the start again. I imagined three hundred and sixty degrees on a protractor as I was led into the room.

Mr. Edenburg and I were dressed in black; he in a black shirt, black trousers and black shoes, and me in black overalls and black rubber boots— the exact opposite from the people in the room. I remember that black and white are opposites and, from somewhere in the back of my mind, I remembered that black and white weren't even true colours, whatever a true colour was. This was something I would take with me to the grave. The people inside the room were busily scurrying around at the last minute as I entered through the door, and Mr. Edenburg put his hand on my arm very tightly. I looked at him, and he looked at me and told me that I looked good without the grey beard and long grey hair.

I told him that I thought I looked twenty years younger, though I didn't feel twenty years younger and, as a matter of fact, I felt like I was three hundred years old and that I had reached the end of a long, long road, and that I was satisfied to have reached the end of a long, long road, but now I know that the road wasn't long at all; it was forgotten. The many years of trying, the many years of walking, the many years of working, the many years of eating, the many years of sleeping, the many years of loving, and the many years of giving, the many years seeing; all of them; all those years forgotten, but inside me.

Mr. Edenburg led me forward to the chair as the last of the people in white left the room. He placed me down, and it felt comfortable to at last sit, and I began to look around me. At a height higher than a very tall man, there was a window and looking out from that window was a whole row of faces I recognised. First, I saw Mother, her face reddened with tears, and next to her was Father, sitting pale faced and frightened, though I don't know why. Next to Father was my sister, who sat staring at Mother and Father for the rest of my life, and next to my sister were the two doctors from the building with the triangle outside— their names escape me at this moment. I wanted to wave to the doctors, but found I couldn't, as, since I had been looking at the row of faces peering out from behind the window, Mr. Edenburg had fastened my arms to the chair by the use of two white leather straps. Next to the two doctors was a face I had never seen, and next to that face was another face I couldn't quite place, either.

I remember I forgot that Mr. Edenburg was busily working his way around my body strapping me into the chair, and it surprised me when he came back into my line of vision between me and the people in the observation room. Mr. Edenburg asked me who I was, and I replied that I was William Kenneth Ian Right, and then he asked me how I felt. I told him that I felt all right, and I can remember asking Mr. Edenburg who the people were that were seated next to the doctors through the observation windows. Mr. Edenburg told me that these people were nothing to worry about and, in fact, were there to make sure that everything went according to plan, and that my every wish was to be carried out perfectly. I eased myself into the chair when hearing this, and it was good to know that my whole family was there watching and that there were people wanting to help me right up to the last seconds of my life.

I was all strapped in, and I thought that this would be like what a rollercoaster ride felt like just before setting off up the steep, steep rail. Mr. Edenburg asked me if I was okay, and I remember getting comfortable in the chair with the straps, moving my body to and fro with tiny little movements to feel totally comfortable. Mr. Edenburg then stopped and looked at me right in the eye, man to man, then, for some reason or other, he brought his open hand to my cheek, patted me twice on the face, and whispered to me that everything would be all right. I leant my head forward as far as I could with the restraint around my neck, and whispered back to him that I knew it would be okay, and that was why I was doing this. He smiled at me, and I placed my head back on the chair's headrest.

At my side was a machine that looked as if it was part of this chair. I looked at the square machine, which, to me, looked as if it did nothing, because I couldn't see it attached to anything else in the room, apart from the chair I was sitting on. It didn't have lights or make a noise or anything that any other kind of machine might do; it just sat there square and white. Hanging from that machine was a long, white tube. Mr. Edenburg lifted up that tube and, at its end, was a long, thin needle. Mr. Edenburg reassured me that this wouldn't hurt too much, and I remember saying to him that I'd had enough hurt in my life and that this little needle was not going to hurt me at all. He pushed it gently, and, I thought, a little too far, into my left arm.

Mr. Edenburg walked to my left toward the door, and I followed him with my eyes as far as they could move to the left, until they hurt and I couldn't see him anymore. Alone at last, I sat there and, for the first time in a long time, heard the ticking of a clock, though I couldn't see it. I stared up at Mother, Father, my sister, the two doctors from the building with the triangle in front of it, and the two people next to them. The seconds ticked on, then, to my surprise, Mr. Edenburg appeared behind the two doctors and rested a hand on each of their shoulders. He then leant forward and his hand disappeared from view; there was a slight hiss from the machine between a tick tock from the clock, and I knew inside me that the liquid had been dispensed from its holder.

Sitting there waiting for the liquid to run its course, to ooze from within its container and run idiotically down the tube and inside my arm, using nothing but the laws of gravity, seems almost surreal to me now. I prayed for God, then I prayed for the meaning of death to be God. I prayed so hard as that liquid instantly ran down the tube, surprising me with its velocity as it entered my left arm through the needle. I could feel the liquid inside me moving around my veins and organs, and around the different parts of my body, and I prayed for God again. I prayed for God to enter my body instead of that murdering liquid.

I looked up at Mother, and she had her head in her hands and, as I looked for Father, my eyes closed for the last time, and I watched the little squiggles like tiny animals under a microscope begin to fade and die like a disease. In a millionth of a second, the last millionth of a second before I died, I sat at the edge of the known universe and traced a timeline back through my life. The grass was green, the greenest I'd ever seen, and the birds were chirping in the trees. I followed that timeline straight to me here. I prayed for God again; prayed for the existence of God. I got something altogether different.

0

Afterwards

From the Journal of William Kenneth Right

JULY 30, 2101

FOR EASE OF READING, I'M GOING TO SPLIT TODAY'S SECTION of my journal into three blocks, as it has been such a tumultuous day in my history for so many different reasons. I am going to split today's writing into past, present, and future blocks. I hope it all makes sense at the end. Today has been a great coming together of time in my life, and I will need to explain it all from beginning to end in the only way I can say it; that means straight from my mind in straight-talking terms. The reason I am addressing you today and did not address you directly in my last section is that today I set the ball rolling on what I consider to be my means of being. Today, it all began, but, without yesterday and yesteryear and the sun... Well, none of this could have taken place. Please, allow me to begin.

THE PAST

In the history books, you can read about the reasons why I had been called back from the dead. It was one of those timelines that, when read from the start to the end, you probably wouldn't believe it, but, then again, which timeline in the past thousand years or so could you believe? Plus, now that I come to think about it, the history of the planet is the most astonishingly unbelievable story ever told, from big bangs and collisions, from dinosaurs to world wars, to collisions and ice ages and floods. I'll try to explain my new timeline from start to finish concerning the most important parts, or even the parts of the past I think are interesting enough to tell you.

The worldwide virus epidemic that began in Central Europe slowly took charge in the countries of Germany, Poland and Austria, and then spread like wildfire across the rest of Europe, culling the population. Doctors and scientists had no idea how to treat this new epidemic, and fear gripped Europe. The whole continent was quarantined, and... Well, we know how well that went, don't we? The links to the U.K. were well established by now, by tunnel and bridge and hover car, and any other means you may think of. The quarantine was a complete failure, as the doctors and scientists had no idea how the virus was spread. So then, the U.K. fell to the virus and, within three weeks, the population had been reported to be ninety-seven percent lower than at the start of the virus. At the same time, the so-called Solar-wind Virus spread east, through Russia and China, having the same devastating effect on the population of these huge countries as it had had in the U.K.

China was, by now, the most powerful nation in the world, and it feared some kind of political or military backlash from the U.S.A. in its weakened state, and, in its paranoia, sent thousands of little parcels of the virus by missile to mainland U.S.A., Central America and South America. This not only doomed the American continent to the effect of the Solar-wind Virus, but it also kicked off the war of wars between the U.S.A. and China, of which the political and nuclear fallout is still being felt today.

It took two months for scientists to realise that the virus had been started by a freak of nature in space, by some kind of passing comet or other, and had been spread by a huge solar wind, which was fanning the disease from space between the sun and Earth.

It was decided that the scientists had to go into space and get samples from the comet to get the virus in its original form, as, by the time it hit Earth's atmosphere, it was too late to study; something to do with the virus' reaction to the oxygen in the atmosphere, although I'm not sure what, but what I do know that it had already taken on its outstanding deadly form by the time it had drifted down from the stratosphere to our atmosphere, so they had to get it in its un-mutated state before they could solve the mystery of finding the cure for it. This took another two months and, as the scientists were busy studying the Solar-wind Virus orbiting Earth, the people on Earth were being massacred by the microscopic space organism.

It took the scientists a total of seven months to identify and be able to treat the virus and, by this time, the world population had been wiped out by an average of eighty percent, from ten billion to around the two billion mark. It was a year of nearly total annihilation for the human race, and it was not something that would be allowed to stand in our way. There were many nations with no political ties after the war, which every country was involved in, one way or another; an unfortunate occurrence, more tied in with the global economy and trade. This war between the main nations of the U.S.A. and China had a devastating effect on the global economy and, ten years ago, the global stock market crashed, sending most of the nations on the planet into a recession never before seen.

So, all these things were playing into my dead hands: the lack of bodies to work, the lack of bodies in the population and, the fact that those countries not still fighting with the US in the war wanted to repopulate. All this happened ten years after my death, so, in the next thirty-odd years, things went from bad to worse for humanity. Nineteen years ago, the war ended between the U.S.A. and China; this then kick started the regeneration of the population of most nations. So it was left to DNA technology to raise the dead from the depths of the state building, and the equivalent state buildings all around the world. We were... I mean, the dead were, there, slumbering through the decades, the saviours of the human race.

THE PRESENT

THIS SECTION TAKES PLACE TODAY. WELL, FROM a point sometime this afternoon. Just to inform you, the time is now 11:48 p.m. I can remember his voice counting down from five to one and, with each number, I was feeling a little more aware of my surroundings and of the doctor's instructions. *Five; you are feeling restless and want to come back to now, gently and with no pain. Four; you can sense that you are back in the current time, and that all is well, and that you are breathing easy where you lie. Three; you can feel your body and your mind relaxing back to the now, and your blood is moving around inside you, and you are calm. Two; you can hear my voice clearly and, inside your mind's eye, you are back in this room with me. One; you open your eyes, calm and relaxed, and you are back in the present with me now, and everything is okay.*

Afterwards

I opened my eyes and saw a certain Doctor Eugene Joseph sitting looking at me on his large leather chair with his calm eyes. He leant over me, unplugging the machine that was gently strapped to my arm, leg and head, monitoring me as I was regressed. I felt good lying there on his black leather couch being someone. The room was vast and dark, which, at first, I thought was odd, but then I remembered through the heat on my skin that it was sometime in the middle of July, and I could see the sunshine trying to break in through the barrier of the window blinds, which had been drawn to aid the ambience and my comfort during my session. I could feel the gentle heat around my body, and the sweet stroking of the air from the fan hanging above our heads. The gentle breeze it caused came in troughs between the peaks of heat, and it was beautiful to feel the nuances of life brush against me.

Previously, I had been regressed nine times, and this was my last session. With each week, I had been drawing on the experiences and thoughts of my previous life. Each time, the clarity was a little more defined, though I'm more than sure it was also a way for the state to keep tabs on how I was feeling and to see if I had any serious side effects, or even any symptoms of any side effects of the procedure. I was, at this moment in time, some kind of state guinea pig. Anyhow, I can remember Dr. Joseph asking me how I felt, and I replied that I felt a little groggy, but okay. The last hourly session had been quite intense for me and, as I was coming to on Dr. Joseph's couch, I was focussing on the huge shelving of books behind his desk, which took up the whole back wall of his office.

I was slowly coming around, gathering my thoughts and regaining my composure. Dr. Joseph agreed with me that it was a very intense hour of regression; in fact, the most intense he had certainly felt with me, and maybe up there with the most intense he had ever guided anyone through.

He then asked if I thought that ten sessions would be enough regression for me, and I said that the last hourly session was very clear and had taken me back over a vast expanse of time from my previous life. The big difference, though, was that I did not experience any painful memories over the death of my wife and my daughter, as I had done the previous two times when regressed over the same situations.

This seemed to me and Dr. Joseph to be a huge positive from this regression session and, in a way, you could call me cured from all that pain and hurt, even though the event took place well over seventy years ago. I thought that we may as well call it a day with the regression sessions, as this was my tenth and, officially, my final session, and I didn't really want to delve any deeper into the past with this technique. Dr. Joseph agreed with me and stated the obvious: he said that I looked really comfortable with the outcome of the hypnotherapy regression sessions and with the outcome of my previous life, and to be honest with me, it did not feel like the me from that previous life existed today in this life.

As I got up from the couch to walk over to the chair in front of the doctor's table, he flicked a switch, and all the blinds in the room simultaneously began to open, allowing the bright sunlight into the room. I felt like I was drowning in the golden light as it flooded up the walls, bouncing off every surface in the room. I couldn't remember the speed of light, but I knew it was fast, and I knew it was in charge of itself. I mean, it didn't obey the rules; it was the rule. I felt a little better now, and the slight dizziness had left me and, to finalise today's meeting with the doctor, and, of course, any contact with the state, I had to sign a declaration.

I took that sheet of paper from him and rested it on my thigh, signing my name with glee on top of that dotted line: William Kenneth Ian Right. Dr. Eugene Joseph then stood from his chair and extended his hand, and we shook cordially. I strolled from his office through the afternoon sunshine glimmering on the thick paint on the corridors of power; it felt good and fine to be free, at last, from the grasp of the state.

Walking through this maze of a building, I was thinking about everything and something, my thoughts careless about which life they were thinking of. One second, I was thinking about my childhood, the second one where I always had that nagging feeling of something else, of there being something not quite right about me or my surroundings, or what was said to me or who I was. I don't know how, but I knew there was something about me, and I just couldn't place the notions that scrolled through my head like cryptic messages from the past. It was like I was dragging a heavy, invisible weight around with me everywhere I went, and with every breath I took and every word I uttered, like everything I in me was trying to remind me of something that had previously happened. I couldn't place it at all, through all those childhood years of not fitting in with the majority of children.

The next second, I was thinking about my mother, dead for over half a century now, dead for as long as she'd nearly existed, and then my thoughts would zoom forward to this life in the school playground, and then back again to the other life randomly searching through the years before this moment, before everything made sense to me. In this life, I was doing everything perfectly; my past confirmed this, and the state had rubber stamped it for me five minutes earlier. I was a man of God, if not a messenger of God, sent to do what I was doing. Instantly, I thought of Lucy again, beautiful Lucy, and couldn't wait to get home to her and hold her and tell her how much I loved her, and then make love to her again and again and again, until her day finally came. That was up to me; in Lucy's life, I was the law of nature and she my subject.

I escaped the walls of the building, and strolled out into the clear blue sky and brilliant sunshine. Above me, wisps of cloud stretched like cotton across a canvas of luminous blue and, all around my head like huge insects, the cars zoomed on their way above the ground. I walked over to my vehicle and sat inside, my chair oozing around me for total comfort. I turned the engine on, and, immediately, the car began to push away from the ground. It growled around me, and I looked above my head through the visor in the roof to find a hole in the traffic. The computer locked onto a gap twelve vehicles down and, with perfect timing, placed me into the space in the air traffic. I can remember feeling absolutely free from everything flying along fifty feet from the ground, and even the simplest of things amused me, like the traffic around me being controlled by the use of computers, and then I allowed my mind to wander again and catch up with its own train of thought.

It was now eleven weeks ago to the day since I'd got the letter from the state that confirmed everything I had been fantasising about all these years. I began that day in the normal way, getting up and drinking coffee, then reading through my web-based mail. I opened my mail first thing every morning before I went out to work and, as I sat reading through my inbox, sipping my coffee, I came to a strange sender, from the office of DNA regression. Immediately, like a giant puzzle, everything slotted into place somewhere in the back of my mind, even though I did not have the parts of the puzzle. I was to report to Doctor Eugene Joseph and, even though that web-based mail did not tell me the purpose of my visit to the DNA regression building, I knew I would be given the answers to all the strange lingering questions that had been bothering me all those years. In the words of Dr. Joseph, I was going to have 'the means to scratch the itch' I had felt for the first eighteen years of my life.

I went to the DNA regression building with an open mind, and sat astounded at the desk of Dr. Joseph as he explained to me the official reason for me being there. After I had died, my body had been burnt. Well, the parts of my body the state had deemed to be unfit for transplant, as I had requested, but my DNA had been placed in cold storage, for want of a better term, in the basement of the building in charge of Special Social Services. This is where Dr. Stuart and Dr. Parmajurantha worked. I can remember, as Dr. Joseph was talking to me, I wasn't looking at him. No, I was thinking about the number three and the symbol, a triangle, which was placed at the front door of the state building of Special Social Services, and on the letterhead sent to me by Dr. Stuart.

It was a perfect thing, everything all in threes: Special Social Services, DNA, the Father, Son and Holy Ghost and, of course, this life, the afterlife and the past life. There were others, if you looked hard enough; my three decrepit rooms I strolled through like a ghost all those years ago and, of course, who could forget the rest of my now-deceased family? Mother, Father, and my sister. Dr. Joseph went on to tell me that I was one of the new members of society. Well, what he meant was that I was a cloned version of myself, taken from a sample of my DNA seventy or eighty years ago in Dr. Parmajurantha's office. Oh yes, all my physical information from my previous life had been stored away by the state for use at a later date and, if I was ever needed again by 'the powers that be', the state only had to stimulate our DNA and grow us back into human beings.

Dr. Stuart laid all this information on me like layers of an onion. I felt more protected the more he told me, and, the more he told me, the more determined I was to carry out my work in this life. Dr. Joseph then explained to me that only certain people were allowed to take part in this procedure, and that there were a few criteria we had to meet. Firstly, we had to have wanted to end our previous life, which, of course, I had. Secondly, we had to have no children, which, of course, I had none of. Thirdly, we had to have permission from the remaining members of our family to agree to the procedure taking place.

The last one surprised me, as I can remember Mother being dead against my decision and, now that I think about it, she must have thought it was in my best interests that I ended my previous life, basically to put me out of my misery. I'm sure, though, that that's why 'the powers that be' are there for us; to help us on our way through life, no matter the decisions we may wish to take.

Dr. Joseph explained to me that it was mandatory for people in my position, the second generation people, as we were now known, to undergo this procedure of DNA regression. He explained that it would do me good, and I can remember that I instantly stated that I wanted to go through with the procedure, as I seemed to have a lot of unanswered questions or thoughts, or things just continually going randomly through my mind. Dr. Joseph stated that this was a small side effect of the process and, at the end of the ten-hour course of DNA regression, I should not be feeling any of these niggling little thoughts. In fact, he said that I would feel the best I'd ever felt, either in this life, or, he joked and laughed, in the last life.

Then Dr. Joseph told me that, after people like me— the euthanasia people— were reborn, 'the powers that be' would start on the millions of DNA samples in cold storage, and that it would be a kind of free for all, and that anyone from anywhere could be reborn again in this time. He also explained that I was one of the first people in this country to be regenerated, and that I should be using the DNA regression sessions well, as they would not be offering them to everyone. I was to be studied for the ten hours of regression, and the data stored and used at a later date for further research in the future.

I had learnt a lot in my eighteen years of life. I realised at an early age that you make your own luck in life, that you should fight for the things you thought were good for you, and, I always knew that honesty was the best policy, but never really understood, until my rebirth, that honesty could be evil, too. It was as obvious as the nose on my face, and yours, too. I mean, all the wars that had ever been fought couldn't be fought if honesty was just a good thing, could they?

Zooming through the sunshine and the shadows cast by the huge cloudscrapers as I made my way towards Lucy in my apartment, I allowed my mind to wander again to the end of the final session, when I recall I walked through those sunlit corridors, through the state's DNA regression building, through the electric doors opening in front of me and closing behind me, with a sense of absolute happiness inside me. Even though I knew that the emotion of happiness was only justified in the years where we lived and breathed and, for the last fifty-odd years, I had not existed, I couldn't wait to get home and tell Lucy all about my last meeting with Doctor Joseph. I was going to call her, but decided against that in case she was taking a nap in the afternoon.

He held the records from my previous existence in his hands, and told me that I would not be allowed to look through them until he was satisfied with me and I was satisfied with myself. I signed myself over to the one hour a week for ten weeks course of DNA regression, to begin the week after and end at least two and a half months later. So this was two and a half months later. Between me working and being God, the weeks flew by. Each week, I learnt a little more about myself and about the work I truly wanted to do. I felt together, and everything made sense; my past, my goals and my present situation. I was a part of something, something eternal.

Arriving home in the late afternoon sunshine, I decided to start the ball rolling with Lucy, though, at that time, I did not know what I was going to do with her. When I got in through the door on the balcony, I could smell her, and went immediately to her. She was exactly the way I had left her. I'll paint the picture for you. She is naked, tied up on a chair I've modified. It didn't take much to do it, as I added extensions from the seat of the chair and the back of the chair so I could tie her up securely. The leather straps that I added to the extensions have silver buckles to secure them, and secure them I did, around her legs and arms, four for each leg and four for each arm.

I tied them tight so I could see the skin bulging around the bonds. Her legs were up in front of her, her knees tucked up under her chin, and her feet resting neatly against her buttocks, her outstretched arms held tightly by the binding on my little modification of the chair. She looked like a letter 'T' in upper case, if you can imagine looking at this 'T', and the top is her arms and the bottom is her legs; not a perfect analogy, but the best I can do at the moment. She had been sitting like this for three days now, and I thought when I saw her that it was time to end it all.

To be honest, I felt kind of sorry for her; her little breasts were sitting there like cushions on her body and, because of the way I had arranged her legs, her pussy was wide to the world, or, I should say, wide to my world. I first made sweet love to her, pumping her hard, nearly lifting the chair from its foundations and, for some reason, I found myself swearing at her, with my sweat dripping over her face. She cried; I came. We didn't speak to each other during the love-making. Well, she couldn't, as I'd bound her mouth, but hey, I still enjoyed it. Then I was thinking about what to do with her, and I could see the fear in her eyes.

First, I got some scissors and cut off the end of her nipples; she howled and cried, but couldn't move. I was her hunter, and she the product of today's society. I then pulled out her toenails with a pair of pliers, and then, with a hacksaw, sawed off her fingers, though, by this time, she had stopped writhing in agony, and I think she had passed out. I cut off her ears next, and threw them on the ground next to her fingers, and then, for some reason, I tried to knock her nose off with a hammer. I failed, and instead had to get a chisel and chisel the thing off. I can tell you, it didn't look good. I untied her from the chair and threw her body onto the floor. With a bigger saw, I sawed off her arms— this was easy— and then, while standing at her side to make the angle better, I sawed off her head, which amused me to no end.

Her body parts were, by this time, making a nice little pile on the floor, and it is amazing how little room we actually take up when are all cut up and tidily stacked away for disposal. The rest of the job was easy; I sawed the lower half of her body just above the pubic hair and, in doing this, the sperm from our love making oozed from her hole. I felt squeamish at this point, and nearly didn't manage to get through the rest of the dissection, but I did, finishing off with her legs, one by one cutting through the tops of where they met the bottom of her body. Suddenly, there she was, all lying on the floor of the spare room, her head beside her legs, her fingers beside her ears and, for amusement, the two halves of her body the wrong way, her breasts below her bellybutton and her nipples... Well, I could only ever have placed them where they finished, one on each eye.

THE FUTURE

When we are not here— I mean in the now, in this moment— there is no pain, no suffering, no hope, no fear, no happiness, no failure, no starvation, no light, no family, no death, no language, and no ideas. There is, quite categorically, nothing around us or inside us or within us when we don't exist. What I think I'm trying to say is that there is no God when we don't exist; God is a concept for the salvation of our souls, but that is the very thing we do not need to save, because our saviour is our demise. I know because I've been there and back. To not exist is a painless Hell.

When we are aware of our lives— I mean alive— we are at the mercy of the cosmos; we are the victims of each second of our life. We are born, we are young and unaware, then we grow up a little, and we become a part of the fabric of our surroundings of the streets we walk down, of the schools we attend, of the stores we shop in, and of our friends' lives. Then we become invincible, but only invincible with the illusion of youth, for time is now beginning to push us over the precipice and, even though the edge of oblivion is there, it is out of sight in the darkness. How slowly we move to be thrown over its edge, but we remain in our own little minds as invincible temples of muscle.

If we are lucky and we manage to reach the next stage of our lives, which I was not in my past life, we become intellectual and thoughtful, consuming the information around us, digesting slowly as if the mind was the mouth to some kind of ethereal stomach, feeding us and giving us hope when, as I only know too well, there is no hope. There is nothing beyond the flesh of the mind or the flesh of the body; we are empty vessels stimulated by random events, convulsing in the slow death of the universe.

Afterwards

So, the challenge is, or even the question is, how do we live? How must we live? To be more exact, the answer is that we must live to the full capacity that our minds allow us to live. I don't mean our minds as in the minds that belong to others, no! What I mean is the deep penetrating mind of existence where each moment is our own, every second meaning something, even if we are only walking, or waking, or washing our hands, or looking at a burning fire.

This is meaning, true meaning, and, when you take all this as a base level of existence and then think of Lucy lying there next door, her body wrapped in a bag, her mind closed, her life and death securely in my hands, well then, let me tell you that God is in me and, as I write this journal for someone else after I pass away for the second time, let me also say the God is within you, too. You only have to see the vast expanse of the nothingness of the death experience to see that the eyes you look from are God's eyes, to see that the feet you walk with are God's feet, the mind you think with is God's mind, and that there is only one question left to answer: who owns who? Is it God who owns us, or us who own God? Do not leave your answer to the hands of chaos; seek and you shall find. Until the next Lucy, *adios amigo*.

Lightning Source UK Ltd.
Milton Keynes UK
08 December 2010

164029UK00002B/28/P